KT-119-516

EARTHFALL

Mark Walden

GALAXY PLUS

First published in Great Britain in 2012 by
Bloomsbury Publishing Plc
This Large Print edition published 2013
by AudioGO Ltd
by arrangement with
Bloomsbury Publishing Plc

ISBN: 978 1471 340161

Text copyright © Mark Walden 2012

The moral right of the author has been asserted

All rights reserved

British Library Cataloguing in Publication Data available

ROTHERHAM LIBRARY &
INFORMATION SERVICES

B52 007 254 8

Printed and bound in Great Britain by
MPG Books Group Limited

For Meg,
who invaded and took over my world

1

The boy ran down the rain-soaked street, weaving between abandoned cars. He crouched behind one of the vehicles and tried to quiet his laboured breath. At first he heard nothing, but then behind the noise of the falling rain he made out another sound—one that in recent months he had learned to fear. The high-pitched whine was getting louder, and that meant the Drones had tracked his scent. The boy forced himself to his feet, pushing the long black hair out of his eyes and set off down the road again. He didn't look back—if there was anything behind him he would rather not know.

He ducked through the broken door of one of the shops lining the street and ran between shelves stocked with now useless electronic devices. Vaulting over a counter at the far end of the shop, he grabbed the handle of a door marked 'Staff Only', silently praying that it wasn't locked. The handle turned and he stepped into the gloom of the room beyond. As the door closed again, he was plunged into darkness. The boy unzipped one of his coat pockets and pulled out a small torch. He played the thin beam of light across the rows of shelves piled high with boxes of all shapes and sizes. Not so long ago, these boxes contained expensive luxuries; now they were just relics of a world that had been lost, probably for ever. He knew that the pouring rain would mask his thermal signature and the telltale sounds of his desperate flight, but it would not make him invisible. He had to keep moving.

He quietly made his way to the back of the storeroom and found the loading bay. To his left he saw the electronic control panel that would once have raised and lowered the rolling steel shutter, and cursed under his breath. He dropped to one knee and tried in vain to pull the shutter up, but without electricity it was pointless—it was locked firmly in place. He froze as the high-pitched whining sound became louder again and he heard the sound of shattering glass coming from behind the Staff Only exit. Fighting a rising tide of panic, the boy looked around the storeroom. He realised, with mounting horror, that heading back through the shop was his only way out.

The boy switched off his torch and slid along the wall in the darkness, trying desperately not to make even the tiniest sound. He stopped as something cold and hard pressed into his back. Turning, he ran his hands over the cool metal cylinder hanging on the wall, feeling a tiny flicker of hope. Then the door to the storefront exploded in a flash of bright green light. He was knocked to the floor by the force of the blast, temporarily blinded by the brilliant burst of light. He lay stunned for a couple of seconds before he was roused by his own terrified voice screaming in the back of his head, telling him to get up; he had to run. He reached for the cylinder and grabbed it, slowly pulling himself to his feet. He froze, not even daring to breathe as something floated through the shattered remains of the door, just a few metres away. It looked like a horrific mechanical jellyfish. The metallic skin that covered the bulbous disc of its body rippled in a disturbingly organic way as clusters of glowing,

2

multifaceted eyes swivelled and twitched, scanning the room. Hanging below its body was a writhing bundle of flexible tendrils, each ending in a vicious, barbed tip. The Drone turned and flew towards him with a piercing screech, its tentacles raised. The boy did not hesitate—he squeezed the handle of the fire extinguisher and the Drone was instantly enveloped in a billowing white cloud of carbon dioxide gas. The boy continued to spray the screeching, flailing machine as he ran past it, heading for the door. He yelped in pain as one of the Drone's limbs lashed out, its razor-sharp tip slashing straight through his clothes and leaving a long gash across his chest. The boy threw the extinguisher at the creature and ducked through the mangled doorway, knowing that he had bought himself a few seconds' head start at best. He leapt over the counter and sprinted through the store and into the street. He took the first turn on his left into a debris-filled side alley, looking over his shoulder as he ran. There was no sign of the Drone, but he heard a piercing, unearthly screech that was immediately answered by several identical calls from nearby. The boy knew that he had to get off the street. The rain was starting to ease and in the eastern sky he could see the first signs of dawn. He might be able to outrun the Drones, but they would call for other hunters and against many he knew he had no chance—not in daylight.

He ran out of the far end of the alley and turned right. If he could just make it the hundred metres to the end of this street, then he would be safe, for the moment at least. From somewhere overhead a low, throbbing rumble made the boy glance upwards before quickly dashing for the cover of another nearby shop doorway. Directly above him a huge triangular vessel, its gleaming black skin pulsing with thick veins of sickly green light, flew low over the rooftops. Beams of bright white light speared out as a series of portals opened on its underside, and swept along the streets below. The boy waited until the vessel had passed directly overhead and then sprinted towards the other end of the street. He knew he had just seconds now; he had seen ships like this one before. Ducking behind a wrecked van that was lying on its side in the road, he pulled a short crowbar from his pack and began levering open the manhole cover beside him. At the far end of the street the vessel banked slowly round before coming to a halt, hovering in mid-air. The boy watched as a hatch opened in the bottom of the triangular craft. A black metallic pod ten metres tall slowly floated down and came to rest on the road below. The boy pushed the manhole cover to one side with a grunt and quickly climbed down on to the rungs of the ladder set into the wall of the concrete shaft below. He started to drag the manhole cover closed behind him as the pod began to open. A huge metallic claw wrapped itself around the edge of the opening and something enormous emerged from the shadows within. The boy pulled the manhole cover shut, his heart racing as he climbed down the ladder. Halfway, one foot slipped out from under him and he fell the last couple of metres, landing on his back in the fetid drain water that ran along the bottom of the tunnel below. He winced in pain, but fought the urge to cry out as earth-shaking footsteps thudded overhead. He held his breath as they got nearer and nearer, the vibrations shaking dust from the

4

tunnel ceiling. The footsteps passed directly above him before receding away into the distance and the boy finally let out a long, relieved sigh.

'Too close,' he muttered to himself under his breath. He reached into his pack and pulled one of the half dozen recently foraged tin cans from inside and inspected it. 'After all that, these had better be the best baked beans ever made.'

The boy trudged through ankle-deep water in the sewers, the light from his torch playing over the crumbling brickwork on either side. He rounded a bend and stopped in front of a gate held shut with a padlocked chain. He pulled out the key that hung on a loop of string round his neck and undid the lock, stepping into the passage beyond, before securing the gate once more. He knew that if they found him down here the chain would make little difference, but it made him feel better all the same.

He walked along the passage and into the chamber ahead of him. There was a large circular cistern, filled with water in the middle of the room and a grate far overhead that allowed at least some of the daylight from the world above to filter down to where the boy stood. He headed up a staircase that spiralled around the cistern, leading to a door marked 'Maintenance'. Using a disposable lighter he lit the gas-powered camping lamp that sat on the shelf just inside the door. He closed the door, then carried the lamp and his backpack over to the table on one side of the room. He sat down on the folding metal chair in front of the table and started to unload the contents of the pack. He looked at the six cans of beans that he had managed to find in the flat above one of the local shops. It was enough for a week, ten days at the outside.

Every day it was getting harder to find food as the Walkers systematically looted for anything edible. Fresh water was difficult to locate too, ever since the taps had run dry. He was starting to wonder if London was still the best place for him to be. Sure, there were lots of places to hide and initially there had been plentiful supplies everywhere, but the Walkers were stripping the city bare and it seemed like there were more and more Drones patrolling every night. If things kept on this way, it was only a matter of time before they caught him.

'Might be time for a holiday in the countryside,' the boy said.

He shook his head with a sigh; he had to remember to try not to talk to himself. At first it had been comforting, but after a while it had made him notice all the more acutely that there was now no one left to answer. He pulled the water bottle from the side pocket of his pack and allowed himself one quick swig. The one advantage of the rain last night was that he had at least been able to top up his water supply. It certainly wasn't mineral water, but it would do. He put five of the tins on the shelf above the table and opened the sixth one, eating the beans cold from the tin with a spoon. When he slept, he dreamt about hot cooked meals, but even though he had managed to find a camping stove on one of his earlier foraging expeditions he rarely had the time or the motivation to use it. He scraped the last of the tomato sauce out of the tin and threw it into the corner of the room, where it joined many others.

The boy slowly pulled off his coat and T-shirt and stood in front of the mirror that hung on the front of one of the storage cupboards, inspecting the gash across his chest. He was relieved to see that the cut didn't seem too deep despite being sore to the touch. He stared at himself in the mirror for a moment longer. He'd lost probably a third of his body weight over the past few months and the slim face topped with long, straight, jet-black hair that stared back at him seemed strangely unfamiliar. Once upon a time he had been teased about his weight by other kids, but now he knew that they would never make fun of him again. If someone had told him back then that he would one day actually miss Simon Haines shouting 'fatboy' at him in the playground, he would have told them they were mad. Now he'd happily put up with it just so he could hear another human voice again.

He opened one of the storage cupboards that lined the room and pulled out a small first-aid kit. He cleaned the wound with an antiseptic wipe and wrapped a bandage round his chest a couple of times to cover it, picking up the slashed and bloodstained T-shirt with a sigh. It looked like he would need to do some clothes 'shopping' soon too. That could wait for another time though. Right now he was exhausted.

The boy lay down in his sleeping bag on top of the inflatable mattress on the other side of the room and picked up the small battery-powered radio that lay next to his bed. For five minutes he slowly rotated the tuning dial with his thumb, listening for any sign of a human voice between the static, but there was nothing, just the relentless white noise that he had been listening to for the past eighteen months. He turned the radio off and closed his eyes. The encounter with the Drone had very nearly been a disaster. He knew that he couldn't afford to make mistakes like that and not for the first time he found himself wondering if he should try to find himself more substantial weapons. At the moment he carried nothing deadlier than a Swiss army knife when he went above ground, but the problem was finding something more useful. For a while he'd carried a baseball bat, but that had just been a pain to lug around. What he needed was something light but effective, a gun ideally, but there were very few of those to be found lying around, especially now that the Walkers had hoovered up anything useful or dangerous for their masters. He'd just have to keep looking, he thought to himself as he slowly drifted off to sleep, and hope that in the meantime he could avoid any more close encounters.

The boy awoke with a start. His dreams had rarely been pleasant since that day eighteen months ago, but this one had been unusually vivid. He'd been slowly walking towards a cliff and could not control his legs. He just kept on taking one step after another, getting closer and closer to the edge. The final, inevitable fall was what had woken him. He opened his eyes and checked the old-fashioned

8

wind-up watch that had replaced his own when the battery had failed a month earlier.

'Whoa, nice job there, Rip Van Winkle,' the boy said, raising an eyebrow. It was ten o'clock at night. He'd slept for nearly fourteen hours. Suddenly he was shaken by a coughing fit that made the gash across his chest flare with searing pain. He lifted the bandage and looked at the wound beneath. The area immediately surrounding the gash was an angry red colour and there were fine green lines just under the skin that seemed to be spreading out from the site of the injury and across his chest.

'Just what I need,' the boy said to himself as he got to his feet unsteadily. He had learned from experience how dangerous an infected wound could be, but he'd hoped that by cleaning and dressing it he would have avoided any complications. He opened another one of the storage cupboards and looked along the shelves of books inside. He'd realised early on that his best chance of living through this was by learning the basic skills needed for survival and so one of the first books he'd looked for was a first-aid manual. Books were easy to find; the Walkers didn't seem to care about them at all and so bookshops and libraries still had full shelves. It was a good job too, because if they hadn't he suspected that he would have been driven mad by boredom long before now. He flicked through the book and made a note of the names of the antibiotics he would need to find. He knew it wouldn't be easy—hospitals and pharmacies were some of the first places that the Walkers had stripped.

He used a piece of duct tape to patch up the tear in the bloodstained T-shirt and pulled it carefully over his head, wincing with discomfort. He slipped his coat on and picked up his pack before opening the door leading to the cistern room. A confused frown appeared on his face as he saw the daylight flooding in through the grating far overhead. He quickly looked again at his watch.

'Oh no,' he whispered.

It wasn't ten o'clock at night, it was ten o'clock in the morning—he'd only been asleep for four hours. Pain lanced across his chest again and he suddenly realised how serious the situation was. If the infection from the wound had already spread that far, there was no way he could wait until nightfall to go out and search for antibiotics. By then he might not even be able to climb the ladder to the surface. The only option was to go topside in daylight, but that was practically suicidal. Another coughing fit came from nowhere and he reached for the railing in front of him to steady himself as the room seemed to spin round him for several sickening seconds. As he fought for breath and the spinning slowly stopped, he knew that he had no choice.

It was really very simple: maybe get killed up there, or definitely die down here, alone in the dark.

2

The boy peered out from the shadows of the storm drain, squinting against the brightness. He waited, listening carefully, but heard only birdsong and the sound of the river meandering past a couple of metres below him. He crept forward out of the culvert and for the first time in months felt the sun on his face. In the past it might have been a wonderful feeling, but now it was doing nothing to stop the clammy chill slowly creeping across his body. He tried hard to ignore the voice at the back of his head telling him that this was more than just an infected wound, that the Drone had done something to him, something bad. He scrambled up the riverbank and at the top lay flat, peering across the park. He normally preferred to use one of the less exposed exits from the sewer system, but today he needed what was on the other side of the park. It was one of the largest hospitals in London—one of the places that he tried to stay as far away from as possible. It was a magnet for Walkers and where there were Walkers there were always Drones. His body was suddenly shaken by another coughing fit and the burning pain in his chest drove him to his feet.

He made for the hospital's main entrance. The doors were open and there were multiple trails of muddy bootprints leading inside. Walkers had definitely been here, but he had no idea how recently. He crept into the gloomy reception area. His own breath seemed impossibly loud as he listened carefully for sounds coming from further inside the building. He heard nothing but the smothering silence that he had become used to over the past months. The boy read the signs on the wall and quickly spotted what he was looking for. He headed off down the corridor to his left, following arrows to the pharmacy. A couple of minutes later he was at the top of a flight of stairs that led down to basement level. He peered into the darkened stairwell and pulled the torch from his backpack. Without any electricity the only light inside the building was what bled in through the windows, but down there it would be pitch-black. He made his way down the stairs, shining the torch on the ground just a metre ahead of him. The muddy bootprints headed towards the pharmacy and the boy realised with a sense of creeping despair what that meant. The pharmacy would be empty.

He continued to follow the signs on the wall and the bootprints on the floor until he arrived at a small waiting area lined with tired-looking plastic chairs and a serving counter sealed by a rolling steel shutter that was set into the wall. Further along the corridor was a door that led into the dispensary area. It had already been forced open, the frame around the lock splintered and cracked. He pushed the door further open and peered inside. There was nothing here. He made his way to the rear of the room, hoping that something might have been missed. He found several shelves still filled with medical supplies, but could not find the antibiotics he needed. He did, at least, find a couple of large plastic tubs filled with painkillers and after popping a couple of pills in his mouth to try to deaden the pain in his chest, he shoved the rest into his backpack. He took several packets of bandages and other dressings and tubes of antiseptic cream, anything that might prove useful in the future. It struck him as odd that these shelves had been left untouched by the Walkers.

Heading back to the counter he looked around for anything that might give him some clue to where he still might be able to find the medication he needed. He spotted an empty trolley off to one side with a clipboard hanging from its handle. He picked it up and read the top sheet of paper. It was a list of medicines to be distributed to various departments of the hospital, and as he read it he saw that the majority of the antibiotics were sent to either the children's ward or the geriatric ward. That made sense—the very young or the very old would be most vulnerable to infection. He just hoped that the Walkers hadn't looted those wards as efficiently as they had the pharmacy.

He hurried back up the stairs, grateful to leave the darkness of the basement, and headed towards the reception area when he heard a sound that sent a chill down his spine. At first it was hard to make out, but slowly it became clearer. It was the sound of marching boots and it was getting louder with each passing second. That sound could only mean one thing: Walkers were coming. The boy looked around desperately for somewhere to hide. He hurried to the glass wall at the front of the reception area and looked outside. There, just a couple of hundred metres away, a column of marching people was entering the hospital car park. Their bizarre assortment of dirty clothes and long ragged hairstyles gave them a dishevelled appearance that was at odds with their strangely

13

disciplined lockstep march. The boy knew that the other thing they would share was a haunting, vacant expression that showed no hint of the personalities they had all once had. There was nothing behind a Walker's eyes, no indication of the humanity that had once been there.

He ran back into the shadows, leapt over the counter and tried to slow his breathing. As the noise of marching feet filled the reception area, the boy could make out another sound—a low, throbbing hum. He wasn't surprised, every group of Walkers he'd seen had been accompanied by Drones, but he'd been very careful to never get this close to a group of them before. Suddenly, as a high-pitched, almost ultrasonic, whine filled the air he felt something he had not felt in months—a bizarre, uncomfortable sensation in his head, like having an itch in the middle of his brain that he couldn't scratch. A second later it stopped and the sound of marching started again as the Walkers headed further inside the building, presumably to continue stripping the hospital of any supplies that they might need. The boy rubbed his forehead as the irritating sensation inside his skull faded. He still had no real idea what it was, but it certainly brought back unpleasant memories of the day all those months ago when the world had changed for ever.

The boy could still hear the Drone hovering somewhere nearby. For some reason it wasn't following the Walkers into the building. In fact, it didn't seem to be moving at all. The boy dared not risk sneaking a peek over the counter to see where it was; he knew all too well that if he could see it, it could see him and that would be a very bad thing indeed. He had learned a painful lesson the previous night about just how dangerous it was to not maintain a safe distance from those floating nightmares. He had no choice but to wait and hope that it would eventually move away.

For several long minutes the boy crouched, praying that the Drone would follow the Walkers further into the building. Just as he was starting to think that he might have to take a huge gamble and make a break for it, the pitch of the throbbing sound from the Drone increased and it began to move. For a few terrifying seconds the noise got louder, but then it began to diminish, heading further away.

The boy took a deep, relieved breath and, without warning, his chest convulsed as another coughing fit struck. He clamped his hand over his mouth, trying to stifle the sound, but it was too late. The hum of the Drone grew louder again as it returned, attracted by the unexpected noise. The boy darted out from behind the counter and sprinted towards the front door, all hope of remaining hidden gone. The Drone rounded the corner behind him and emitted a horribly familiar shriek as it spotted its prey. A short black tube on the top of the hovering creature swivelled towards the boy, and with a flash and a crackle fired a searing bolt of green light at him. The boy dived forward through the doorway as the energy blast struck the glass directly behind him. The huge sheet of toughened safety glass shattered into millions of tiny pieces all around the boy. He leapt to his feet and began running across the car park, dodging between the rows of dusty, abandoned vehicles as the Drone streaked across the reception

15

area in pursuit, the low throbbing sound of earlier replaced by an angry-sounding whine.

As the boy reached the street, his chest felt like it was on fire, his lungs fighting desperately to suck in enough air. Another green energy bolt sizzled through the air, missing the boy by inches as he frantically zigzagged down the street, trying to keep the creature from drawing a bead on him. He ran behind a bus and down the pavement, cutting left into the entrance of a shopping mall. The sound of the pursuing Drone was getting louder all the time and he knew with a horrible certainty that he was never going to be able to outrun it. He certainly couldn't fight it; his only choice was to hide. He ran into the central atrium of the shopping centre. Escalators on both sides led up to the upper levels and the whole area was brightly lit by daylight pouring in through the glass dome roof high overhead.

The boy was blown off his feet as a large map displaying the mall's floor plan exploded right next to him. He tried desperately to force himself to his feet, still deafened by the ringing in his ears, but could do little more than roll over and crawl backwards, away from the hovering Drone. There was nowhere to run; he knew he was finished and he couldn't help but feel a strange sense of relief that at least the nightmare he had been enduring for all this time was now, finally, over. As the Drone floated towards him, the boy closed his eyes, hoping that it would at least be quick.

The rattling sound of automatic gunfire suddenly filled the air and the boy's eyes flew open in shock as the Drone was struck by a hail of bullets that tore ragged holes in its metallic skin and sent oily dark green liquid spurting out. It floated backwards, screeching as another burst of fire struck it and knocked it out of the air.

The boy watched in astonishment as a figure in black body armour and wearing a gas mask walked down one of the nearby escalators. The soldier raised an assault rifle and fired one last burst into the wounded creature, leaving it twitching on the ground in a pool of green fluid. Walking towards the boy, the soldier pulled off the gas mask. Beneath the mask was a girl who looked to be about the same age as him with long dark brown hair, pale skin and blue eyes. She offered him a hand and pulled him to his feet.

'My name's Rachel,' the girl said in a soft Irish accent, a tiny smile tugging at one corner of her lips, 'and we've been looking for you for a long time.'

The boy just stood there, his mouth agape. It was the first time he'd heard another human voice in over eighteen months. The boy's mouth moved silently, struck dumb as he tried to pick which question to ask out of the thousand that had just sprung into his head.

'So, do you have a name?' the girl asked.

'Sam,' the boy replied in a whisper, feeling a dizzying combination of overwhelming relief and utter bewilderment. 'Sam Riley.'

'Pleased to meet you, Sam,' Rachel replied, rolling the dead Drone over with her boot. 'Now tell me, can you run?'

'I think so,' Sam replied. His head was still ringing from the explosion that had knocked him off his feet and the wound on his chest still felt like it was on fire, but he knew they had to get out of

17

here as quickly as possible. Where there was one Drone, there were bound to be others. A sudden roaring sound made them both look up at the glass dome as a huge triangular black object cruised past overhead.

'Good, because we need to move fast or we're both dead.'

3

Sam ran after Rachel as she sprinted out of the mall and turned left, heading down the street outside.

'Come on,' she shouted over her shoulder. 'We have to get out of here before that ship drops a Grendel on top of us.'

'What's a Grendel?' Sam asked, struggling to maintain the same pace as the sprinting girl.

'You don't want to know,' she replied as she hurried to the side of the street and pressed close to the wall of a café so that she could peek round the corner into the next street. 'Trust me, if you'd met one you'd understand.'

'Big thing, giant metal claws?' he said, thinking back to his narrow escape the previous evening.

'Thought you said you'd not seen one.'

'I haven't, but I think I very nearly got to meet one yesterday.'

'Then you're lucky to be here at all. Come on, this way looks clear.' She set off round the corner.

'Listen, thanks for rescuing me back there,' Sam said as he followed after her. 'You saved my life.'

'You're welcome,' Rachel replied, suddenly

stopping with one hand raised. Her voice dropped to a whisper. 'But we're not out of this yet.' She raised the assault rifle to her shoulder as Sam heard the familiar sound of approaching Drones coming from somewhere ahead of them.

'Should we hide?' Sam asked, taking a step backwards.

'No,' Rachel replied with a frown, lowering the rifle. 'There's only one way we're getting out of here in one piece now that we've got a drop-ship looking for us and it's in that direction. Ever used one of these?' She pulled a pistol from the holster on her hip and offered it, grip first, to Sam.

'Errr . . . no,' Sam replied, taking the gun, 'not something we covered in school.'

'Well, consider this your first lesson,' she said with a serious expression. She took his free hand and positioned it so that he had a firm two-handed grip on the pistol, then raised his arms until he was holding the weapon at eye level. 'Safety's off, round in the chamber, point it at what you want to hurt and squeeze the trigger. Just try to make sure that I'm not standing between you and whatever that is.'

'OK,' Sam said nervously. 'Am I allowed to ask how you know all this?' She couldn't be more than a few months older than him, but she carried herself like a professional soldier.

'Answers later, fighting now,' Rachel replied as she raised her rifle and began advancing down the street.

Sam swallowed. The strong survival instinct that he'd acquired over the past few months was screaming at him to run. It would be easier just to find the nearest manhole cover and scurry back to his hiding place in the sewers. *Like a rat*, he thought to himself, feeling a flare of unexpected anger. Maybe it was meeting this girl and realising for the first time that he wasn't actually alone or maybe it was the reassuring weight of the gun in his hand that was somehow giving him courage, but as he stood there he made a decision.

'You know something? You're right,' he said, taking a deep breath. 'Enough running.'

Sam followed Rachel down the street, weapon raised, as the sound of the Drones got louder and louder. Suddenly, fifty metres away, three of the hovering silver creatures floated out of a side street. Rachel didn't hesitate, opening fire the moment that she saw them and hitting the lead Drone with a lethally accurate three-round burst. Sam took a deep breath and aimed at one of the other two as they turned towards him and Rachel, training their energy weapons on them. He squeezed the trigger and with a loud bang the pistol bucked hard in his hands. The shot went high, hitting the wall behind in a puff of orange brick dust. He lowered his aim slightly and fired again. This time the bullet struck home, hitting the Drone in the left-hand side of its silvery body just as it fired its own weapon. Sam felt a burst of intense heat in his side as the Drone's shot flashed past him, punching a hole in his coat and searing the side of his chest. He yelled out in pain, but kept firing, hitting the Drone again and sending it spinning backwards, spraying green liquid in all directions. Rachel switched her fire to the last Drone and brought it down with two short, controlled bursts of fire. She advanced quickly on the wounded Drone as it floated drunkenly through the air, screeching angrily. She finished it off with a single shot and it crashed to the ground.

'Nice shooting,' she said with a slight smile and a nod.

'Thanks.' Sam felt slightly breathless as the adrenalin coursed through his body. 'Beginner's luck, I guess.'

'I don't think luck's got anything to do with it,' Rachel replied. 'Some people are just better at this than others. You know, I think you're going to fit right in with the rest of the gang.'

'Gang?' Sam asked. 'You mean there are more people like you?'

'Who do you think taught me how to do this?' she said, as she set off running again. 'Don't worry, you'll get to meet the others soon enough. Assuming we get out of here in one piece, of course.'

They continued their headlong dash through the deserted streets, Rachel in the lead with Sam close behind. As the adrenalin subsided, Sam began to feel the throbbing pain in his chest again. He was struggling to keep up with Rachel as she sprinted ahead of him, his breathing becoming more and more laboured. He started to slow and Rachel glanced back over her shoulder, slowing her pace to match his.

'Are you OK?' she asked, sounding concerned, as he jogged up alongside her.

'Not really,' Sam said with a frown. 'I'm not feeling so good to be honest. I had an unpleasant encounter with one of those things and it cut me. I think the wound's infected. I was trying to find some antibi—'

'Show me,' Rachel said, cutting him off.

'Now?' Sam asked.

'Right now,' she snapped back.

Sam pulled his T-shirt up to reveal the bloodstained dressing round his chest. The fine network of veiny green tendrils had spread even further and were now clearly visible all around the bandaged area. Rachel carefully lifted up one edge of the dressing and looked at the wound beneath.

'When did this happen?' she asked quietly.

'Last night,' Sam replied.

'How many hours ago?'

'I don't know eight, maybe nine,' Sam said. 'Why is it so important?'

'Because you should be dead,' Rachel replied, looking him in the eye. 'I've never seen anyone survive a Hunter sting for more than a few minutes. This doesn't make any sense.'

'A Hunter?'

'Yeah, those floating silver jellyfish things that we just met. We call them Hunters.'

'I've always called them Drones, you know because of the sound they make.'

'Drone, Hunter, whatever, the point is that once they sting you you're dead inside five minutes,' she said, still inspecting the gash across his chest. 'There's no way you should even be standing up, let alone running around.'

'Well, I'm not dead yet,' Sam said with a slightly pained smile, 'but I've felt better.'

'We've got to get you to Stirling right now,' Rachel said, gently replacing the bandage. 'He needs to see this. It's not much further. Do you think you can keep moving?'

'Do I have a choice?' he said, pulling the T-shirt back down.

'Not really. Come on.'

She set off, jogging down the street again at a slightly more forgiving pace, and Sam did his best to keep up. As he ran, Sam couldn't help but be distracted by how odd the streets looked now. Normally, his trips to the surface had been brief and made under the cover of darkness, and as he saw what the abandoned city looked like in daylight for the first time he had to admit that it freaked him out. The café with tables still neatly arranged on the pavement outside, the coffee cups sitting upon them now filled with rainwater. The delivery lorry with its tail lift down, surrounded by damp, sagging cardboard boxes. A pushchair sitting empty in the middle of the pavement.

'Two more minutes,' Rachel said. 'Not far now. Once we get to . . .'

The rest of her sentence was lost as the front of one of the buildings twenty metres ahead of them exploded in a shower of shattered masonry and billowing grey dust. Both Sam and Rachel staggered backwards, shielding themselves from the falling debris as an unearthly roaring howl came from somewhere within the cloud. Rachel grabbed the sleeve of Sam's coat, her eyes wide with fear.

'Grendel,' she whispered. 'Run.'

Sam didn't need to be told twice and the pair of them sprinted back down the road.

'This way!' Rachel snapped as she dashed down a side street. Sam could feel a steady thudding vibration running through the ground beneath his feet as a huge, dark shape began to emerge from the swirling cloud of dust behind him. He quickly glanced over his shoulder just before he

23

rounded the corner.

'Oh my God,' he said quietly, slowing to a standstill as he finally saw what it was that had caused the devastation. It was ten metres tall and covered in interlocking black armoured plates, their smooth, oily surfaces glistening in the light. Like the Drones it seemed to be neither wholly organic nor mechanical, but instead something in-between. Visible beneath the plates were flexible sheaths of thick, segmented cables that bulged and contracted like exposed muscles. The creature's head hung low between the enormous carapaces on each shoulder, the red, glowing eyes set deep within its monstrous horned skull narrowing as it sighted its prey. It roared again, its mouth opening wide to reveal row after row of razor-sharp teeth. The creature advanced, sweeping a car in the middle of the road aside with one of its enormous claws, the talons tearing through the metal with ease. It began to move more quickly, ripping fresh chunks out of the road surface with each step of its huge clawed feet. Sam felt like a rabbit trapped in headlights as the Grendel thundered towards him, its blade-tipped tail sweeping from side to side. Rachel grabbed the sleeve of his jacket and hauled him into the side street, almost pulling him off his feet and snapping him out of his terrified daze.

'We have to find cover,' she yelled as they ran headlong down the street.

'Couldn't we just hide inside one of these buildings?' he shouted back as the Grendel rounded the corner behind them.

'That thing would tear the place down around us. We have to get to the rendezvous point now!'

They raced between abandoned vehicles as

the Grendel thundered after them, swatting the cars and vans aside as if they were toys. As they reached the end of the side street and ran out on to a wider road, Rachel glanced behind them and without a word dived into Sam and knocked him flying. A split second later a car spun through the air over their heads, before cartwheeling across the road and smashing through a shopfront with an explosive crash. They scrambled to their feet and kept on running as the Grendel emerged from the side street, relentlessly gaining ground on them. Sam fought to ignore the painful spasms in his chest, knowing that if he slowed down the monstrous techno-organic creature would be on him in seconds.

'There!' Rachel yelled, pointing down the street ahead of them. Sam looked for what she was pointing at and spotted a familiar sign, a red ring with a blue bar across its centre bearing the single word 'Underground'. At that precise moment he couldn't think of anywhere else he'd rather be.

'Head for the entrance!' Rachel yelled as she unslung the assault rifle from her back, turned towards the charging Grendel and opened fire. She fired three short, controlled bursts at the creature's eyes and it slowed, raising one of its huge metal claws to shield its face, while still advancing. Rachel continued to fire, backing steadily towards the Tube station entrance. The Grendel raised its other arm and, without warning, a black tendril shot from an orifice on the back of the creature's wrist and speared towards her. The tentacle swatted the rifle from her hands before viciously whipping back into her shoulder, knocking her off her feet and sending her flying. Sam stopped his headlong dash towards

25

the Underground entrance and ran back towards Rachel as, her face contorted in pain, she forced herself up on to her hands and knees. The tentacle whipped back through the air towards her and mercilessly slammed down on her back flattening her to the ground again before snaking round her ankle and starting to reel her in. Rachel clawed at the road surface, trying to find something to grab on to as Sam sprinted towards her.

'Don't be stupid! Get out of here!' she screamed at him.

'I told you, I've had enough of running,' Sam hissed through gritted teeth. Rachel gasped in pain as the mechanical tendril tightened its grip on her leg.

'There's no point in that thing getting both of us,' she snapped. 'Just go!'

Sam ignored her and pulled the pistol from the waistband of his jeans. He took careful aim at the thick, black tentacle and fired. The bullet pierced the glistening segmented skin, sending gouts of thick, dark green ichor splashing across the tarmac. The Grendel gave a deafening enraged roar and yanked its arm back, dragging Rachel to within just a few metres of its feet. The creature took a single step towards Sam and Rachel, towering over them, raising its free arm high above its head, claws extended for a killing blow. Sam closed his eyes.

There was a whooshing sound from somewhere behind him and then an incredibly loud explosion. Sam felt a wave of intense heat as he was lifted from the ground and sent flying backwards through the air before slamming down hard, flat on his back, all the wind knocked out of him. For a few seconds he lay stunned before slowly opening his

26

eyes. He forced himself to his feet and surveyed the scene before him. The Grendel was trying to get up, hindered by the fact that the mangled, smouldering remains of the arm that had been dragging them in for the kill lay severed and twitching on the ground, several metres away. Thick oily liquid spurted from the jagged remnants of the wounded creature's shoulder. Rachel was lying face down on the road. She wasn't moving. Sam staggered over and gently rolled her on to her back. She was bleeding from a cut just below her hairline and as he tried to lift her up her eyes fluttered open, her brow furrowing into a pained frown.

'What happened?' she groaned.

'I did,' a voice said from behind Sam. Walking towards them was a tall, muscular boy wearing combat trousers and a white vest. His hair was a mass of dreadlocks, held back from his face by a black headband covered in tiny white peace symbols. He pulled a short tubular object from his backpack and pulled on each end, extending it and locking the two halves in place, before raising it to his shoulder. A similar object lay discarded on the ground a few metres behind him.

'Jay, your timing is, as usual, perfect,' Rachel said as Sam helped her to her feet.

The Grendel had finally regained its balance and now took a single faltering step towards the three of them.

'You might want to get behind me,' the boy called Jay said as he squinted through the sights mounted on the top of the rocket launcher. 'I'm gonna put this thing down for good.'

Sam and Rachel moved out of the way as Jay waited two seconds for the gentle bleeping from the launcher to change to a continuous tone, indicating a positive lock on his target. He took a deep breath and pressed the firing button on top of the launcher. The rocket streaked across the thirty-metre gap that separated them from the wounded Grendel and struck the creature squarely in the centre of the chest. The explosion tore it to shreds, smouldering chunks of its armoured, black shell scattering in all directions.

'So much for tall, dark and ugly,' Jay said, a broad grin spreading across his face as he discarded the spent launcher. 'Now, I reckon we should get off the street before any of his friends show up, 'cos I'm out of rockets and that little firework display is going to attract every Hunter within ten miles.'

In the distance they could hear the low throbbing roar of one of the black triangular drop-ships growing louder.

'You'll get no argument from me,' Rachel said as she picked her rifle up off the road. 'Jay, this is Sam, Sam this is Jay. It's short for Jacob, but I only call him that when he annoys me. Which is surprisingly often.'

'Pleased to meet you, Sam,' Jay said with a broad grin, shaking his hand. 'So you're the last one of the Doc's little lost sheep, huh? Been looking forward to meeting you.'

'Is anyone actually planning to tell me just what the hell's going on at some point?' Sam asked.

'Stirling will explain everything,' Rachel said, turning to the nearby entrance to the Underground station. 'Come on, let's go.'

The three of them ran towards the stairs leading down into the darkness as one of the giant black triangles soared past overhead, a bright rectangle of white light appearing as a hatch opened in its belly. The last thing Sam saw as he ran down the stairs was dozens of Drones pouring out of the hatch, swooping down towards them.

'Hunters,' Jay said as he ran down the steps behind Sam. 'We need to get into the tunnels fast.'

Behind them they could now hear the buzzing hum of the Drones as they searched for their prey.

'Won't they just follow us down here?' Sam asked as they ran through the abandoned station concourse, navigating their way through the darkness using only the meagre light provided by their torches.

'Probably,' Rachel said as she jumped over a ticket barrier, 'but this is our territory. They're not catching us down here.'

'Yeah, man,' Jay said, 'we're like rats. We know all the best hiding places.'

Sam climbed over the turnstile and followed Rachel down a stationary escalator, heading into the bowels of the abandoned Tube system. The noise of their headlong dash through the station seemed unbelievably loud to Sam and the buzz of the hunting Drones somewhere behind them was getting closer all the time. They kept running until they reached one of the station platforms, which stretched away into the darkness on either side of them.

'This way,' Rachel said as she jumped down from the platform and on to the track. 'If we can make it to Sanctuary Twelve, we can hole up and wait for the Hunters to give up the search.'

'How far is that?' Sam asked. He was finding it increasingly difficult to catch his breath.

'Half a click,' Jay said, pointing his torch down

at the track. 'Watch your step—last thing we need now is a broken ankle.'

'That's half a kilometre,' Rachel said, rolling her eyes. 'You'll have to excuse Jay—little bit too much Call of Duty. Thinks he's a soldier.'

'We're all soldiers now, Rach,' Jay said. 'You as much as anyone.'

The three of them hurried down the pitch-black tunnel in single file, Jay in the lead, Sam in the middle and Rachel bringing up the rear. They'd gone a couple of hundred metres when the sound of the Drones behind them changed subtly.

'They're in the tunnel,' Rachel said. 'You see the hatch yet, Jay?'

'No, not yet,' he replied, a slight note of concern in his voice for the first time.

'It's got to be close,' Rachel whispered.

'I know,' Jay replied, 'but I'm telling you I can't see it.'

Sam heard a gentle click from behind him as Rachel thumbed the safety catch on her rifle to the off position.

'Wait . . . I got it,' Jay said, hurrying towards a hatch set low in the wall twenty metres ahead of them. Sam heard Rachel's relieved sigh, and they followed Jay down the tunnel. Rachel pointed her torch at the hatch as Jay turned his off and shoved it into his pocket.

'Give me a hand,' Jay said, tugging at the hatch's rusty metal locking handle.

Sam grabbed on to the bar and pulled hard and, with a mechanical groan of protest, it slowly began to move. A moment later the lock disengaged and the two boys hauled the hatch open with a creak.

'Quick, inside!' Rachel hissed, glancing over her

30

shoulder. The noise of the Drones was very close now. It sounded like they would be on them in just a matter of seconds. The three of them clambered through the hatch and Rachel closed it behind them, pulling the locking bar back into position before turning off her torch. They crouched in the darkness, hardly daring to breathe as the whine grew steadily louder and louder. For a moment Sam thought that they'd stopped outside the hatch, but then the buzzing sound started to diminish as the Hunters continued further along the tunnel and all three of them let out long relieved sighs.

'Too close,' Rachel said, turning her torch back on and directing its beam down the corridor that led away from the hatch. 'OK, we should be able to follow the secondary tunnel network all the way from here to the Sanctuary. Once we're there we'll have to wait a while before we head back to Central Command. We can't take the chance that any Hunters in the tunnels might follow us back there.'

They continued down the dark, twisting passageways for another twenty minutes. Jay and Rachel appeared to know exactly where they were heading, but Sam was hopelessly disorientated after just a few minutes. He'd thought that the layout of London's sewers was complicated, but the network of maintenance tunnels that they were now navigating was even more intricate and convoluted. If you got lost down here, he realised, you might just never see daylight again. Eventually, they arrived at a short flight of concrete stairs that led up to a heavy metal door. Rachel released the two bolts holding the door shut and pushed it open. Sam followed her inside and found himself in a room containing a bunk bed and a battered old armchair. On a table nearby was a kerosene lamp, which Rachel quickly lit. Hanging on the wall above it was a detailed map of the tunnel system surrounding them with various locations circled in red pen.

'Cosy,' Sam said with a wince as he felt the pain in his chest flaring again. 'Reminds me of home.'

'We've got bolt-holes like this set up throughout about a quarter of the tunnel system,' Rachel said, gesturing at the map on the wall. 'We're expanding the network all the time. Idea is that you should always be near somewhere you can safely hide for a while.'

'As long as you don't mind eating this rubbish,' Jay said, taking a foil-wrapped package from a locker mounted on the wall and tossing it across the room to Sam.

'What's this?' Sam asked.

'Twenty-four-hour, general-purpose operational ration pack,' Jay said, taking another one from the locker and tearing it open, 'as once issued to Her Majesty's armed forces. Looks better than it tastes and it looks terrible.'

'Do you ever stop thinking about food?' Rachel said with a sigh as she took off her backpack and sat down in the chair.

'Thanks,' Sam said, putting the ration pack down on the table, 'but I'm not really hungry at the moment. In fact, to be honest, I'm exhausted. I think I might just . . .'

Sam gasped, clutching at his chest, and dropped to his knees as his body was engulfed by a sudden fresh wave of nerve-searing pain.

'Sam!' Rachel yelled, leaping to her feet and

32

catching him as he toppled over. She lowered him gently to the floor.

'What's the matter with him?' Jay asked. He came over and knelt down beside them.

'Hunter sting,' Rachel said, lifting Sam's T-shirt to show the bandage round his chest. The green tint to the veins leading away from the wound now extended almost to his waist and their colour was significantly darker than it had been earlier.

'What do you mean?' Jay asked, looking confused. 'When did he get stung?'

'Last night—least that's what he told me,' Rachel said. 'I know, I know,' she added, seeing the expression on Jay's face. 'I have no idea how he's lasted this long. Listen, I was hoping that we could stay here for an hour or two, but we have to get him to Stirling now. Hunters or no Hunters.'

'Rach, I hear you, but you know as well as I do that even the Doc can't help you if you get stung. No one can.'

Sam groaned, his face contorting as a fresh wave of agony swept through his body. Each breath was excruciating. He was vaguely aware of Rachel and Jay's voices, but they were muffled, sounding like they were coming from somewhere distant. He felt himself slipping away from wherever those voices were coming from as the last of his strength faded and the world turned black.

4

Eighteen Months Earlier

'Come on, Sam, time to get up.' Ellen Riley rolled up the blind in her son's bedroom, filling the room with sunlight.

Sam groaned in protest, pulling the duvet over his head.

'It's Saturday,' he moaned. 'Can't I just stay in bed?'

'You promised me that you'd tidy your room this morning and if you don't do it now you won't have time before going to the cinema with Ben. So, it's your choice—you can stay in bed if you want, but I'm not taking you to his house until you've got this room sorted.'

Sam lay in bed, listening as his mother went back downstairs. He stuck his head out from under the duvet and looked around. Yesterday, it had seemed like a pretty good deal, but now, in the cold light of day, it didn't feel like quite such a reasonable arrangement. His bedroom looked as if a highly localised but extremely powerful tornado had passed through it. Video games were piled up, discs out of their cases, dirty clothes lay scattered on the floor, a pile of discarded comic books lay next to the bed and countless dirty mugs and glasses covered every flat surface. It was, even by his elevated standards, a spectacular mess.

'This is going to take hours,' he groaned to himself.

He climbed out of bed and staggered across

the landing to the bathroom. He turned on the shower and stepped inside, the torrent of hot water washing away the last of his morning drowsiness. He ran his fingers through his wet hair and felt the five-centimetre-long scar that ran across the back of his skull. He had no memory of the surgery that the scar was a relic of but he understood its significance. Since he was little he'd suffered from epilepsy and the device that had been implanted in his skull was to control the neural electrical storms which caused it. He'd had no seizures since and, although the procedure had been experimental at the time, it appeared to have been a remarkable success. He had to go for occasional check-ups, but otherwise he barely even knew it was there. His parents had told him about it just over a year ago and explained that he'd been extremely lucky to be one of the first people to receive the implant. Everything had been fine up until recently when he'd started getting really bad headaches that seemed to always start around the same area as his scar. His parents had been very worried and they'd taken him for a scan, but it had turned out that everything was OK. He'd just needed to take some anti-inflammatory pills and the headaches had faded away. He hadn't had a headache for a couple of weeks now, but that didn't stop his parents fussing over him.

Sam threw on a pair of jeans and a black T-shirt before heading downstairs to get some breakfast. He passed his older sister coming up the stairs.

'Morning, midget!' she said with a grin. 'Are you actually getting slightly shorter every day or is it just me?'

'Very funny, Jess,' Sam muttered, 'but still not as

35

funny as you getting dumped by Greg.'

'He didn't dump me,' Jess snapped back. 'It was a mutual decision.'

'That's not what he's telling everyone,' Sam said, grinning to himself.

'What do you mean?'

'Oh, nothing,' Sam said over his shoulder as he walked into the kitchen. 'You might want to check Facebook though.' His grin widened as he heard his sister running up the stairs to her bedroom and slamming the door behind her, almost certainly heading straight for her laptop.

'Will you please stop teasing your sister?' Sam's mother said. 'She's really upset about Greg, you know.'

'She started it,' Sam said. 'It's not my fault she can't take a joke.'

'Just leave her alone,' his mum replied, frowning.

'OK, OK,' he said as he took a carton of orange juice out of the fridge. 'Where's Dad?'

'In his study. Something came up at work and he's been on the phone all morning. Don't disturb him.'

Sam nodded as he poured himself a glass of juice.

'I'm going over to Aunty Carol's for a couple of hours this morning and I want that room done by the time I get back. Understood?'

'Yes, boss,' Sam said with a cheeky grin.

'Too right I'm your boss,' she replied with a smile, picking up her handbag and checking her watch, 'and don't you forget it, young man.'

She kissed him on the top of the head as she headed out of the kitchen and towards the front door. Sam finished his juice before reluctantly heading back upstairs. He could hear the frantic clattering of the keys on his sister's laptop as she updated all her friends on the ongoing soap opera of her love life. As he walked across the landing towards his room and the Herculean task that awaited him within, he noticed that the door to the study was ajar. He heard his father's voice and he stopped for a moment, listening to the hushed but urgent-sounding telephone conversation.

'I know that, James,' his dad said, 'but it's just too soon. If they're already intra-lunar, then we've got what ... hours? Minutes maybe? I knew we should have rolled the latest batch out sooner. We had enough data, the kids are fine, but now it's too damn late.'

Sam frowned as he heard his father talking. There was a note of panic in his voice that he had never heard before.

'I don't know, James,' his father continued, 'I really don't. You saw what happened at Inshore; you've seen what they're capable of. If this is what it looks like, then this is going to be something on a totally different scale. I have a horrible feeling that it's going to be much, much worse.'

Sam had no idea what his father was talking about, but it had to be something to do with work. His dad never talked much about what he did. It involved the military and computers, but that was as much as Sam knew. A few times Sam had caught glimpses of the stuff that his father was working on but it had just been meaningless screens full of schematics and equations that gave no real clues.

'At this point I don't think that there's anything we can do,' his father said, 'except wait and see what happens. There are plans in place—let's just

37

hope that we don't have to use them. I suppose we'll all know soon enough. Yeah, you too. I'll speak to you later, James, hopefully. Thanks.'

Sam heard the phone bleep and crept away from the study door, heading for his bedroom. He couldn't help but be curious, even slightly worried about the conversation he'd just overheard, but he knew that his dad might be angry if he realised that he'd been eavesdropping. He was halfway across the landing when his dad walked out of his study, frowning.

'Have you seen your mum, Sam?' he asked.

'Yeah, she just left. She was going to Aunty Carol's. She said she'd be back in a couple of hours,' he replied.

His dad sighed and rubbed his temples. 'OK, I'll ring her on her mobile. Listen, I don't want you or Jess going anywhere today, OK?'

'But I'm supposed to be going over to Ben's later, Dad,' Sam moaned.

'Well, you'll have to cancel. Something's come up.'

'Is everything OK, Dad?' Sam asked. He'd never seen his father look so worried before. It was worse than that, Sam thought to himself, he almost looked *scared*.

'Yeah, it's fine. Just a bit of a crisis at work,' he said.

'OK, I'd better get on with tidying my room, then,' Sam said, nodding towards his bedroom door.

'Yeah, that sounds like a good idea,' his dad replied, sounding distracted as he pulled out his phone and tapped at the screen.

As Sam walked into his bedroom he heard his

dad speaking to his mum.

'Hi, honey! Listen, I need you to come home right now ... Yeah, I know, but this is really important. I have to go in to the office. Something's come up. I know ... I know, but this is urgent. Yeah, look I realise it's not fair and, yes, I'm sure Carol is going to be cross with me, but I need you to come home and look after the kids.'

The rest of the conversation between his parents was inaudible, but there was no hiding the fact that something weird was happening. Whatever was going on, it couldn't be any worse than having to tidy this lot up, Sam thought to himself. He dug through the mess on his desk, hunting for the remote control for the television in the corner of his room. He turned it on and switched to one of the music channels, so he would at least have something to listen to while he tidied up. He began to pick up his dirty clothes from the floor and dump them into the laundry basket, humming along with the music. A few minutes later, he heard the front door opening and closing and his mum calling for his dad. Over the music from the television, he could just make out the muffled sounds of their conversation downstairs. Then the telephone started ringing in his dad's study. Sam heard him hurrying up the stairs to answer the call. Then he heard the front door slam and the sound of a car starting. Sam looked out of the window and saw his dad pulling away from the drive at speed. Suddenly the music stopped as downstairs his mother switched channels on the satellite receiver and the pop video was abruptly replaced by a newsreader sitting behind a desk with a slightly bewildered expression on her face. The bottom half of the screen was taken up by a caption that read *Breaking News—Unidentified Object Over London.*

'... still unclear as to the exact nature of this unidentified object, but reports are coming in from all over the world of similar objects appearing above major population centres, and tracking stations say that these mysterious devices do, in fact, appear to be extraterrestrial in origin. We're going live now to Martin Staples outside Buckingham Palace.'

The picture changed to a reporter standing in front of the Buckingham Fountain, surrounded by people who were all staring and pointing at something above them.

'Extraordinary, chaotic scenes here as police continue to clear the immediate area beneath the object ... hovering several hundred metres above St James's Park.'

The camera panned slowly upwards and Sam's mouth dropped open.

'Oh my God,' he whispered.

The object, too big to fit on the screen all at once, was a giant black disc several kilometres in diameter, its curved underside covered in an array of hundreds of enormous segmented parabolic dishes. The edges of the dishes glowed with a pulsing green light, which seemed to ripple outwards in waves from the centre of the disc.

'Eyewitnesses report that the object simply dropped out of a clear blue sky and, with no other obvious explanation, there is only one question everybody here is asking. Could this really be our first contact with an extraterrestrial civilisation?'

The view changed to another shot from a camera further away, which showed the true scale of the vast disc now casting a shadow over central

London. Its upper surface was covered in towering blocky structures surrounding a single, needle-like central spire, which reached high into the sky. The dark surfaces of the towers were covered in pinpricks of the same green light that illuminated the dishes on the underside. There was only one word that Sam could think of that could possibly be used to describe it . . . *alien*.

'Twitter just exploded!' Jess said breathlessly as she dashed into Sam's room. 'Everyone's going on about something really weird happening in London.'

Sam didn't reply—he just pointed at the TV.

'As you can see,' the reporter continued, 'at its widest point, it stretches from Hyde Park to Waterloo station, a distance of, I would say, at least three kilometres. There has been no sign of activity anywhere on the disc and, as yet, no official word on the government's response to this developing situation.'

'What on earth is that?' Jess asked, her eyes wide with surprise.

'There's nothing *on Earth* like it,' Sam replied. 'I think that's the point.'

'We've just been informed that the prime minister is currently meeting the COBRA emergency response committee at an undisclosed location,' the newsreader continued. The newsroom, visible through the glass behind her, was frantic with activity. 'We're also hearing that similar discs are appearing in the skies all over the United Kingdom and the rest of the world. It is unclear, as yet, if these . . .'

Suddenly, the image of the disc on the screen flared with light as the central spire on the top of the vessel lit up with an intense white light and a single beam of energy streaked upwards into the sky. Moments later the dishes on the object's underside lit up, the dim green glow replaced with an intense, bright green light. Sam winced as his skull was filled with a pulsing, high-frequency whine. He shook his head as the volume of the sound increased and he started to feel a strange pressure building inside his head. He clapped his hands over his ears, but it made no difference. He gasped in pain as the screech got louder and louder. Then, just as it felt like his head would burst under the pressure, the sound stopped as abruptly as it had started.

Sam removed his hands from his ears warily and watched on the television as the lights around the dishes on the bottom of the disc faded back to their previous dim level. Suddenly, Sam noticed something odd about what he was seeing on the screen. The newsreader had fallen silent and was now simply staring at the camera with a glassy-eyed vacant expression. Behind her the previously bustling newsroom had fallen silent, and the men and women who had been dashing frantically around just a few moments earlier now stood immobile, like statues.

'Did you hear that?' Sam said, turning to Jess. His sister didn't reply. She was staring at a point on the wall, no sign of any emotion on her face, just the same trance-like expression as the silent woman on the television.

'Jess!' Sam snapped. 'What's wrong?' He grabbed her shoulder and shook her gently but she did not respond, an occasional slow blink the only sign that she was even awake. He waved his hand in front of her eyes, but her focus never shifted. Sam ran out of his room and down the stairs, two at a time.

'Mum! There's something wrong with Jess!' he shouted as he ran into the kitchen. His mum was on the sofa at the far end of the room, staring at the television, and as Sam approached he felt the first fluttering twinge of panic in his stomach. She wasn't, he realised, watching the television at all; she was staring at it, her face frozen and emotionless too. Sam knelt down in front of his mum, put a hand on each of her shoulders and shook her gently. His mother's head rocked backwards and forwards, but there was still no flicker of awareness in her eyes.

Sam stood up, fear replacing panic. He took the phone out of its cradle on the countertop and quickly punched in his father's mobile number, but the call wouldn't connect. He didn't even get his dad's voicemail. He hung up and dialled Aunt Carol's number as he'd always been told to do if there was an emergency when his mum or dad weren't around. The phone rang a dozen times before he heard his aunt's voice on the other end.

'This is Carol Burton. I'm afraid I'm not available at the moment, but if you'd like to leave your name and number I'll . . .'

Sam hung up without leaving a message. There was something seriously wrong and he needed help *now*. He took a deep breath and dialled 999. He stood listening as the phone rang and rang at the other end. He waited, watching as the second hand on the kitchen clock swept around the dial once, then twice. There was no answer.

'What's going on?' Sam whispered to himself.

Suddenly, there was another burst of the skull-splitting, pulsing screech and Sam dropped the phone, wincing in pain. This time the painful howling was quickly replaced by a lower frequency, a throbbing hum. Sam bent down to pick up the phone before looking over at his mother. He gave an involuntary gasp of shock as she stood up and turned towards him.

'Mum, are you OK?' he asked. She did not reply, her face still frozen in a neutral, emotionless expression. Moments later she started walking straight towards him.

'What's the matter?' he demanded. 'Why won't you answer me?'

She walked past Sam and out of the kitchen, oblivious to his presence. He followed her into the hall and saw Jess walking down the stairs, her eyes empty and distant. His mother opened the front door and walked silently out on to the drive. Sam grabbed Jess's arm as she passed, but she kept walking, slowly dragging him towards the door. He tried to hold on to her, to stop her somehow from leaving the house, but she pulled relentlessly away from him.

'What are you doing? Where are you going?' Sam yelled as he finally let her go, and she silently followed their mother through the front door. He chased after them, watching with a growing sense of horror as they walked down the drive and towards the road. This had to have something to do with the low, throbbing sound that seemed to fill the air around him. But if that was true, why had it not affected him in the same way?

Sam ran ahead of his mother, before turning to face her, his arms stretched wide, trying to block

44

her path. Rather than slow her pace she simply walked round him, as if he were an obstacle to avoid. Sam kept moving, trying to block her path again, but it was a futile effort. Whichever way he moved, his mother just changed direction. Jess walked past and Sam quickly realised that trying to stop both of them would be impossible. He followed them, fear and confusion gnawing at his gut.

'What the hell?' Sam whispered to himself as he stepped out on to the pavement. Dozens of people were walking down the street, all with the same vacant expression and all heading in the same direction. Sam watched as his mother and sister joined the procession, merging silently with the flow. He followed them, not knowing what else to do. They were being driven somewhere and wherever that was he had to go with them to try to keep them safe and find out what was going on. As he continued down the street, Sam began to realise something else, something deeply disturbing. There were now crowds of people filling the road ahead of them as more people walked out of driveways and side streets, but he still hadn't seen a single person who seemed to be aware of what was happening.

'Can anyone hear me!' Sam yelled at the top of his voice, almost screaming. There was no response, just the sound of a huge crowd walking in perfect silence. There was something deeply unsettling about seeing such a mass of people and yet not hearing a single murmur of conversation. There was no laughter, no shouting, nothing. As the crowd got larger, Sam struggled to keep both his mother and his sister in sight. They made no effort to stay together and began to drift apart as more men, women and children joined the tide. He realised that before long he was going to have to choose who to stay with, who to follow. Instinctively, he wanted to follow his mother, but she was an adult; she would be more able to look after herself. Jess on the other hand was only a couple of years older than him. He couldn't stand the thought of her suddenly snapping out of this sinister trance somewhere unfamiliar, frightened and alone. He pushed through the crowd towards her, taking her limp, unresponsive hand in his as their mother slowly disappeared from view. Sam had never imagined that it would be possible to be surrounded by this many people and yet still feel so hopelessly alone.

For the next hour, Sam walked along beside his sister as the ever-growing torrent of people flowed towards their destination. The people surrounding him and Jess were of all ages, shapes and sizes. Some were wearing work uniforms, some were in their nightclothes, a few of them were even naked. Babies or children who were too young to walk were being carried by adults who Sam assumed were their parents but might, for all he knew, just have been the people who were physically closest to them at the time. What was most unnerving was the fact that, just like the adults, none of those children made any sound. Not a single baby was crying.

After a while it began to rain and Sam trudged along, still holding on to Jess's hand tightly, feeling cold, wet and miserable. He had been walking for several hours and he was starting to feel thirsty and tired. If any of the people around him felt the same way, they weren't showing any signs of it.

46

He couldn't afford to stop, though. He knew that there was no way he'd ever find Jess again in the crowd, even if he only rested for a few minutes. He trudged on wondering how much longer he could keep going. There was still the low-pitched throbbing that had now just become background noise, but there was also a higher-pitched buzzing that seemed to be getting louder all the time.

Suddenly, three objects flew out from an adjoining street and shot down the road towards them, flying just a few metres above the heads of the crowd. Sam had never seen anything like them; they looked like some kind of flying mechanical jellyfish, with bunches of long dark tentacles writhing below their floating silver bodies. He felt an irritating tingling sensation in his skull and without warning the entranced mass of people all stopped their relentless march in perfect unison. The silver creatures hovered in the air about thirty metres from Sam and Jess. Sam let go of his sister's hand and stood perfectly still, staring into the distance, hoping that he looked just like the blank-faced people surrounding him. Somehow the same primal instinct that was making the hairs stand up on the back of his neck told him that he did not want to attract their attention. After a few seconds, sections of the crowd began to break away from the main group and head off in different directions. He waited as the crowd dispersed in front of them, barely daring to breathe as the silver creatures floated towards him. A few seconds later Jess turned smartly to her left and he followed suit, walking along behind her as she joined a group that headed down a side street nearby. Sam resisted the urge to look back over his shoulder as they walked away, fearing that the slightest sign of independent thought might be enough to alert the creatures that he was not under the same spell as everyone else.

They walked for a couple of minutes before arriving at the entrance to a large storage depot. Sam followed behind Jess as she walked inside. Rows and rows of people were lying on their backs, next to each other on the concrete floor of the barn-like structure. They all had their eyes wide open, staring vacantly at the ceiling. Jess and Sam followed along to the end of one of the rows and Sam took his place next to her as she lay down on the cold, hard floor. Sam glanced around as he lay down. There were none of the silver machines in the room as far as he could tell, but he could still feel the tingling in his head, which he assumed meant that they must be somewhere nearby. He lay there in silence; the only sound he could hear was the gentle breathing of the hundreds of people lying around him. A few minutes later the odd itching inside his skull faded away and he lifted his head from the ground, slowly looking around. The floor was filled with people, all lying motionless, their arms and legs straight, their eyes shut. He sat up and gently shook Jess by the shoulder but, as he had feared, she did not respond. Just like everyone else in the room it was as if she had been switched off.

'OK, Sam, think,' he whispered to himself. 'What do you do now?'

His options were limited. Jess wasn't going anywhere right at this moment, but there was no way of knowing when the people around him might get back on their feet and start walking once more. If he wasn't there when that happened, he knew he'd probably never see Jess again. He decided to check what was going on outside. Only then would he know if it was even possible for him to try to get his sister out. There were no windows on this floor of the building, but a door on the far side of the room had a 'Stairs' sign on the wall beside it. He stood up and carefully picked his way between the dormant bodies, heading for the exit. Looking back across the room, he felt the hairs on the back of his neck prickle at the sight of the dozens of unconscious but strangely stiff bodies, all lying in neatly ordered rows. He shuddered involuntarily and stepped through the door, creeping quietly up the stairs, ears straining for any sign of the return of the sinister silver machines.

The upper floor was filled with empty offices and the only light in the gloomy space was coming from the monitors on the desks displaying the open documents and web pages that had been suddenly abandoned. Sam walked into one of the offices and looked out of the window. It was getting dark outside and the rain was heavier. The streets below were empty; there were no signs of life, either human or alien.

'You're certainly not from around here, are you?' Sam whispered to himself as he looked at the giant vessel that hovered over central London, clearly visible from here, despite the fading light. As he watched, he saw several smaller shapes, illuminated by green light, drop from the underside of the larger ship and then shoot off, flashing through the sky above the city rooftops. It felt ludicrous, but the more he looked at the huge floating object and thought about the bizarre events of that day, the more he was forced to admit to himself that the most likely explanation was that it was the work of an extraterrestrial intelligence. That still did nothing to explain what it was that these visitors had done to the people downstairs or what their future intentions might be. Sam feared that whatever they were planning it was nothing good.

He walked back to the desk in the room and sat down in front of the keyboard. He clicked the icon on the computer's desktop and opened the browser. He was half expecting an error message, but the internet connection still seemed to be working. He spent nearly an hour looking for signs of life online, but there was nothing. The last posts on any of the forums or blogs he visited were startled reactions to the arrival of the alien vessels all over the planet, but then there was silence. It confirmed one thing, Sam realised as a chill ran down his spine: whatever had happened to everyone, it hadn't just happened here in London. It was the same everywhere—this was global.

He put his head in his hands, rubbing his temples, fighting to control the rising tide of panic that he could feel in his gut. He told himself to stay calm, that everyone might wake up in the morning and that the intentions of the extraterrestrial visitors might not be as sinister as they appeared. Or it could be just as bad as it seems, said a nagging voice in the back of his mind, and you're going to die, frightened and alone.

'Stop it!' Sam said to himself, standing up and slamming his hands down on the desk. He couldn't afford to panic; he had to think. Not just for his sake, but for his sister as well. He had to come up with a plan and hope that if he could get Jess far enough away from the city then whatever influence the aliens were exerting over her would fade and perhaps she might wake up.

'Great, so all I've got to do now is work out how exactly I'm going to get an unconscious fifteen-year-old zombie girl out of London,' Sam said with a sigh. He couldn't carry her any distance and even if he could figure out how to drive a car the roads were all blocked with abandoned vehicles. He realised that, unless she woke up from her current brainwashed state, he really only had two options. Either he stayed with Jess and waited for her to wake up or he left her here and tried to find somewhere safe to hole up on his own. It was an impossible choice.

Sam suddenly became aware of a low throbbing rumble that seemed to be getting gradually louder and louder. He hurried to the office window and saw that one of the smaller objects that had dropped from the bottom of the main alien vessel was heading in his general direction. He watched as the dark triangular object grew larger and realised with a growing sense of horror that it wasn't just heading in his *general* direction—it was heading straight towards him! He ducked below the window, just as a bright, white light flooded the office. He crawled across the carpet, towards the door, as the building's windows rattled and the white light swept back and forth across the offices. At the top of the stairs leading down to the warehouse area, he looked back over his shoulder just as the window exploded inwards in a shower of glass. Now he could hear another sound: the high-pitched whine of the silver jellyfish-like creatures that had shepherded them

51

into the building earlier. Three of the creatures floated in through the broken window and glided towards the desk, their writhing tentacles reaching out and gently caressing the computer keyboard and monitor. Sam realised now what he'd done. Somehow, his attempts to find signs of life on the internet must have attracted the creatures' attention and they had traced the network activity back to this location—which meant that now they knew that somebody here wasn't really quite as asleep as they were supposed to be.

He hurried down the stairs as the three drones spread out, searching the offices for their prey. He reached the bottom of the stairwell and was just about to open the door that led back into the warehouse area when a noise from the other side made him freeze in his tracks. There were more of the creatures in there! He risked a quick glance through the glass panel in the centre of the door and saw several more creatures gliding between the rows of sleeping people, illuminating each of them in turn with a single burst of bright green light. He glanced back up the stairwell and felt a chill as he realised that he was trapped.

Silently heading back up the stairs Sam saw a small window, but wasn't sure if he'd even be able to squeeze through it. He unlatched it and opened it, wincing at the loud creak from the hinges. He leant out and looked down. It was quite a long drop to the alley below, but there was a drainpipe within arm's reach that he should be able to climb down, assuming he could first get through the window. He turned round and sat on the narrow ledge before pulling himself backwards through the window with a grunt. He reached out and had just managed to get one hand round the pipe when the door at the top of the stairwell exploded in a flash of green light.

Sam dragged himself further through the window, trying desperately to free one of his legs so that he could get a foothold on the pipe without falling. He glanced inside, just in time to see one of the creatures floating through the smouldering remains of the door at the top of the stairs and then turning slowly towards him. The creature let out a high-pitched shriek and a dark orifice set in its shining carapace flared with green light. Sam grunted as he dragged himself free of the frame and swung away from the window, clinging desperately to the drainpipe, feet scrabbling for purchase on the wall. A second later the entire window disappeared in an explosion of green light and a wave of concussive force smashed into him, swatting him off the pipe and sending him flying. Sam felt a stomach-wrenching instant of free fall before he slammed down into a pile of abandoned cardboard boxes and rubbish sacks in the alley below. The impact knocked the air out of his lungs and he lay there for a couple of seconds completely winded before rolling over on to his knees and forcing himself to his feet with a pained gasp. He looked up at the hole in the wall above. There was another screech from inside and the creature floated out through the smoke. Sam felt a surge of energy as adrenalin flooded his body. Ignoring the pain he turned and ran, his animal instinct to flee now fully in control. He sprinted out on to the main road and turned left, with no clue where he was going other than away from those silver creatures. He ran on to the bridge over the river that he and

Jess had crossed earlier, suddenly feeling horribly exposed. He felt his blood run cold as the air was filled with a deep throbbing roar and a huge black, triangular shape passed low overhead.

Sam looked up and the last thing he saw was a blindingly bright green flash somewhere above him. Then he felt a sensation, like a giant hand picking him up and flinging him spinning through the air, then a sudden impact with freezing cold water and, finally, nothing.

Sam dreamt of his family. They were sitting with their backs towards him on a white wooden bench in the middle of a field of green grass. He walked towards them, but with each step his feet felt heavier and heavier until finally he could not move at all. He stood and watched as Jess and his mum and dad slowly got to their feet and turned to face him. He felt a surge of terror when he realised that they had no faces, just smooth featureless sheets of skin where their familiar features should have been. He tried to turn, to run, as these faceless creatures walked towards him, but it was no good; he was frozen in place. They moved to surround him on three sides, each standing just a metre away. In perfect unison they each reached up with both hands and grabbed the skin below their jawbones, pulling the featureless skin of their faces up like someone removing a mask. Beneath was a void filled with green light that intensified as they each began to make a high-pitched shrieking sound. Sam began to scream as they stepped towards him.

He woke with a start, the scream dying in his throat, replaced with short, ragged breaths as he felt a dizzying moment of disorientation. He was dimly aware that his legs felt cold and that everything hurt, as if his entire body was just one giant bruise. He slowly opened his eyes and lifted his face out of the dirt. He was lying on the mudflats beneath a bridge, his legs still in the river. There was a low throbbing rumble coming from somewhere nearby. A tiny but urgent voice in his head told him he had to move, had to find somewhere to hide, but all that Sam wanted to do was lie there and rest for a while. He tried to fight through the cotton wool inside his head and remember where exactly he was and how he'd got there. He had a vague feeling that there was something really important he had to do. He frowned as the pieces slowly started to reassemble themselves until his memory of the past day came flooding back in one overwhelming burst. He dragged himself out of the water and across the mud before pulling himself up into a sitting position, his back against the crumbling masonry of the bridge. He sat there in silence as the roar of the alien vessel's engines faded away into the distance. He stretched his legs and arms, relieved that, although he was bruised and battered, at least he didn't seem to have broken any bones. The right-hand side of his face and his right arm were quite badly burnt, the skin blistered in places and he could feel exposed patches of skin on his scalp where some of his hair had singed away. He had a long gash in his right thigh and his ribs on that side hurt when he took a deep breath. His T-shirt was shredded and he'd lost one of his trainers, but he

55

didn't really care because, against all the odds, he was still alive. He had no idea how long he'd been unconscious. The pale grey light of dawn lit up the sky now and, given that it had been night-time when he had escaped from the creatures in the warehouse, he knew that he must have been out for several hours at least.

He slowly climbed to his feet before trudging through the sticky mud and up the riverbank to the pavement. He examined the surrounding buildings, trying to get a sense of where he was. There were no familiar landmarks to help him orient himself so he set off along the path, following the river upstream. It was slow-going, his burnt and battered body protesting at every step. All the while he listened out for any sign of the silver creatures or alien aircraft that had attacked him the previous night. It was clear now that whoever the mysterious invaders were they were extremely hostile and he suspected that he would not have such a lucky escape if they found him again.

He rounded a bend in the river and saw a small row of shops on the other side of the road. He walked across the street and headed into the sporting goods shop halfway down the parade. The lights were still on inside the store and he made his way down the aisles searching for new clothes and shoes. He found some tracksuit trousers, a T-shirt and a hooded top and began to take off his filthy, damp clothes. As he pulled off his mud-encrusted T-shirt, he caught a glimpse of himself in one of the full-length mirrors that were dotted around the store. It was not a pretty sight. He was covered in cuts and bruises and the right-hand side of his body was an angry red colour where the heat of the blast from the alien ship's weapon had scorched his skin. He put his hand to his head and ran his fingers over the patches of wiry burnt stubble that were all that remained of his hair in places.

'Great,' Sam said with a tiny smile. 'I didn't think it would be possible, but I actually *do* look worse than I feel.'

He carefully pulled on his new clean clothes and was surprised by how much better it made him feel. He walked to the back of the store and looked at the display of trainers covering the back wall. The single shoes on display were no use to him and so he headed through the door with the sign reading 'Staff Only'. Shelves stacked with boxes filled the room on the other side and Sam quickly found a new pair of trainers in his size. He headed back through the shop, looking for anything else that might come in useful. He picked up a lightweight backpack and slung it over his shoulder and then stuffed half a dozen packs of sports socks and a water bottle inside. He did a quick search of the store, but there wasn't much else that was going to be of use to him. He was just about to leave when he spotted a rack on the far wall. He walked over and took down one of the baseball bats from the display and swung it experimentally through the air.

'Better than nothing,' he said with a nod.

As he walked out of the store, bat in hand, he smiled at the sign telling him that all shoplifters would be prosecuted.

He spent the next half an hour checking out the various shops on the street and helping himself to anything that he thought might come in handy. A portable radio, a torch and a dozen packs of batteries from a hardware store. Painkillers and dressings for the gash in his leg from a chemist. Bottled water, sandwiches and biscuits from a convenience store. By the time he continued his journey upriver, the painkillers were kicking in, the food he'd found had silenced his growling belly and he was actually starting to feel slightly better. Now all he had to do was find his sister.

Sam walked for an hour before spotting the bridge that he and Jess had crossed the day before. He crouched down behind a low wall and waited for several minutes, watching and listening for any sign of the creatures. Once he was satisfied that the coast seemed clear he made his way cautiously over the bridge towards the storage depot. Halfway across, he found the impact crater from the blast that had thrown him into the river. A two-metre section of stone wall was missing and there was a massive tear in the pavement through which he could see the water of the river below. Sam realised just how lucky he'd been. If he had been caught in the direct blast he would probably have been vaporised where he stood. He continued across the bridge, moving as quickly and quietly as possible. A minute or so later he was outside the door to the warehouse. He waited for a moment, ears straining, before taking a deep breath and turning the handle. It took a moment for his eyes to adjust to the darkness inside, but then he saw the one thing that he had been silently praying he would not. The cavernous warehouse was completely empty. Where once there had been dozens of people lying in neatly ordered rows, there was now just a bare concrete floor. His sister was gone.

Over the weeks and months that followed, Sam learned the hard way what it was going to take to survive in this new world. The first time he had seen a group of Walkers he had approached them in broad daylight, hoping in vain that he might spot his mother or sister. He hadn't spotted the silvery Drone that was accompanying the group until it was almost too late. He soon realised that any group of Walkers working on dismantling or stripping buildings of anything useful invariably had a Drone watching over them. For months, he would find a place to hide, from which he could scan the faces of the enslaved people with the pair of compact binoculars he'd found. He never saw anyone he even recognised, let alone any members of his family. After a while, he gave up looking. It was risky getting that close to a Drone and he knew his luck would run out at some point. Eventually, he started going out of his way to avoid Walkers altogether. More and more Drones seemed to be patrolling the empty streets and it was getting harder and harder to avoid detection. That was when he discovered the sewer network. It wasn't the most pleasant way to travel around, but it was at least safer than walking the streets. In all that time, he'd never seen a single person who wasn't a brainwashed zombie. He'd once heard what he thought was gunfire in the distance, but that was it. It had given him some hope that he might not be the only person left with free will. He never heard it again.

Over time, he became adept at moving around the city undetected, as he learned the layout of the sewers and started to only venture out on the streets at night. He even made a more permanent home for himself in a maintenance room next to one of the giant sewer cisterns. His focus shifted from daily scavenging to longer-term survival and he began to read any book that he could loot from abandoned bookshops or libraries that might contain useful information. It was the books that kept him from going crazy with loneliness; it wasn't the same as having people to talk to, but it was the next best thing. His life became a never-ending cycle of furtive looting and foraging, always hungry, always scared, but still alive. There were times when he teetered on the brink of despair, but he never gave in to it. Instead he just got smarter and faster, managed to stay just one step ahead of the Drones. There was no alternative really; it was that or simply curl up and die.

5

'Any improvement?' Rachel asked as she looked down at Sam's deathly pale face. He lay on a camp bed with a drip feeding into one arm and a dressing covering the wound on his chest. The fine tracery of pale green veins still covered his torso.

'Same as yesterday,' the boy kneeling beside Sam's bed said as he removed the blood pressure cuff from Sam's arm. He had a bushy mop of blonde hair, wore a pair of thick-rimmed spectacles and his thin face bore an expression of tired resignation. 'He's not getting any worse, but he's not getting any better either. Stirling's running some tests, but I get the impression that he's as puzzled as the rest of us. He just does a better job of hiding it.'

'OK, thanks, Will,' Rachel said with a sigh. It had been three days since she and Jay had brought Sam back with them and he had been in a coma ever since.

'I'll let you know if there's any change, Rach,' Will said, pushing his glasses up his nose. 'But I'm afraid that it's just a case of wait and see at the moment.'

'I suppose you're right,' she replied. 'I'm not known for my patience, though.'

'You know, I had heard that about you,' Will said with a lopsided grin.

'Visiting our patient again, I see,' a voice with a deep Scots accent said behind Rachel.

She turned to see Dr Iain Stirling walking across the room towards them. He was tall, with short grey hair and a neatly trimmed beard. His brow was furrowed by the slight frown that never seemed to leave his face. Rachel had heard rumours that some of the others had seen him smile, but she wasn't sure she believed it. He was also the reason that she and the others were still alive.

'Yes, Doctor Stirling,' Rachel replied with a nod. 'Will was telling me that Sam's condition hasn't changed.'

'I heard,' Stirling replied, taking the clipboard with notes attached to it from the foot of Sam's bed. 'I also heard that William thinks I am hiding my own ignorance of what is happening to young Mr Riley and that I don't really understand

61

it at all.'

'I didn't mean . . .' Will said quickly.

'Oh, you're quite right, William,' Stirling said. 'I really don't know how he's managed to survive this long. Besides which, there's nothing wrong with concealing one's own ignorance. I just wish you did a slightly better job of concealing yours occasionally.'

Rachel tried very hard not to laugh at the sudden look of embarrassment and mild indignation on Will's face. Stirling pulled a pen light from the pocket of his lab coat and gently lifted one of Sam's eyelids, shining the light into first one eye and then the other.

'Pupil dilation is still good,' Stirling said, 'which hopefully means that there hasn't been any neurological damage.' He pressed lightly on one of the green veins covering Sam's chest. 'The spread of the toxin appears to have halted, but I'm still not sure why, or how he managed to resist its effects for as long as he did. Unfortunately, I lack the equipment I need here to really try and get any detailed answers as to what's going on inside Mr Riley. I do have a theory that might explain it, but I need to speak to him to be sure.'

'Do you need me to draw any more blood?' Will asked.

'No,' Stirling replied. 'I've completed my tests. I'm afraid that all we can do now is wait for our patient here to wake up.'

'I should go,' Rachel said. 'Jackson wanted me on the range ten minutes ago.'

'I'll let you know if his condition improves,' Will said as he walked with her towards the door.

Behind them, Stirling looked down at Sam.

'What did you do to him, Daniel?' he whispered under his breath.

Suddenly Sam convulsed, his back arching off the bed and his arms thrashing wildly.

'Help me!' Stirling yelled at Rachel and Will as he fought to hold Sam down. They ran over to the bed just as Sam's eyes flew wide open, staring at the ceiling. He let out an unearthly howling scream. Will lay across his legs while Rachel and Stirling took a firm hold of an arm each, trying to pin him to the bed.

'Good God,' Stirling said, staring wide-eyed at Sam's chest. The green veins that covered his torso were vanishing as they watched, retreating rapidly towards the site of the original wound. Within just a few seconds the traces of the toxin had almost completely faded and Sam relaxed, settling back on to the bed, his eyes closed again and his breathing ragged.

'What happened?' Rachel asked, eyes wide with amazement.

'I have no idea,' Stirling replied, shaking his head and relaxing his grip on Sam's arm. 'I've never seen anything like it.'

Moments later Sam's eyes fluttered open and he looked up at Rachel with a confused frown.

'Morning,' Rachel said with a worried smile.

Sam lifted his head from the pillow and looked slowly around the room.

'Hate to sound corny,' Sam said after a few seconds, his voice croaky, 'but I have to ask. Where am I?' The room he was lying in had bare concrete walls with no windows and was lit by fluorescent lights protected by wire cages mounted on the ceiling. There were a couple of other camp beds

63

against the opposite wall and at the far end of the room was a long bench that was covered with medical equipment.

'Safe,' Rachel said. 'Don't worry.'

'Safe, that's good. You're real too. Also good.'

'I'm happy to say that, yes, I am in fact one hundred per cent real,' Rachel said as Sam lifted his head from the bed and looked around. 'You had us worried for a while there.'

'Indeed you did, Mr Riley,' Stirling said. 'How are you feeling?'

'Like I got beaten up,' Sam said with a slightly pained smile. 'By a gorilla.'

'Well, you appear to have made a truly miraculous recovery,' Stirling said with a slight frown. 'The problem being that I don't believe in miracles.'

'How long have I been out?' Sam asked, rubbing his eyes.

'Three days,' Rachel said.

'Really?' Sam said. 'I don't remember anything after we headed down into that Tube station, to be honest.'

'You passed out just after that,' Rachel said. 'Me and Jay managed to get you back here in one piece, but you've been unconscious ever since. It's nice to see you with your eyes open again.'

'Allow me to introduce myself,' Stirling said. 'I'm Doctor Iain Stirling and this is my assistant, William, and we've been looking after you for the past few days.'

'Hello,' Sam said, 'and thank you.'

'You're quite welcome. Now, if you don't mind I'd like to take a look under here,' Stirling said, pointing at the dressing on Sam's chest.

64

'Help yourself,' Sam said, letting his head fall back on to the pillow. Stirling carefully peeled back the dressing.

'How extraordinary,' he said as he examined Sam's injury. The wound, which had been showing no signs of improvement just a couple of hours ago, had now fully closed and scabbed over, as if it had been healing for days.

'That's impossible,' Will said, shaking his head.

'Clearly not,' Stirling replied, raising an eyebrow. 'William, would you be so kind as to take another sample of Mr Riley's blood for me. I believe that I might have some more tests to run after all.'

'Of course,' Will said. He picked up an empty syringe from the tray on the table next to the bed and turned towards Sam. 'Is it OK if I just . . . ?'

'Go ahead,' Sam said, extending his arm. He winced slightly as the needle went in, watching as Will drew a small quantity of blood. 'So how far did you and Jay have to carry me?' he asked Rachel as Will busied himself with taking the sample.

'A few miles,' Rachel replied, sitting down on the edge of the bed. 'It could have been worse—at least you don't weigh *that* much.'

'Thanks,' Sam said with a smile. 'I think.'

'You're welcome,' Rachel said. 'There's not many of us left with minds of our own, so we kinda have to look out for each other, you know.'

Will finished taking the blood sample and Sam sat up in his bed, holding a tiny square of gauze to the pinprick in his arm. He watched as Will took the sample tube over to Stirling who was seated at the long bench. He took a pipette and placed a single drop of Sam's blood on to a glass slide, which he then put under a microscope.

65

'So this is the rest of the gang,' Sam said quietly to Rachel, nodding towards the others.

'Some of them,' Rachel said. 'Don't worry, you'll get to meet everyone soon. They're all very keen to meet you. It's been a while since we found a new recruit.'

'Recruit?' Sam asked. 'You make it sound like I've joined the army.'

'Actually,' she replied with a half smile, 'you kinda have.'

An hour later Sam was sitting on the edge of his bed, pulling on his battered boots as Dr Stirling walked back into the room.

'Now, you must promise to take things slowly,' the doctor said as Sam finished tying his laces and slowly stood up.

'I told you. Honestly, I feel fine,' Sam said. 'In fact, I feel fantastic.'

'Be that as it may,' Stirling said, 'you are still recovering from the effects of a toxin that has proven invariably fatal to all of its previous victims. Until we have a clearer understanding of why you have not suffered the same fate, I would like you not to exert yourself. You don't want anything to interfere with your full recovery.'

'I understand,' Sam said with a nod, 'but I've not spoken to another human being for a year and a half. I thought that I was the last person on earth that hadn't been turned into a mindless zombie, so there's no way I'm just going to lie here in bed. I want to go and meet the others.'

'Of course,' Stirling said, 'that's perfectly understandable, but if you begin to feel unwell again or even if you just start to get tired I want you to come back here immediately. Agreed?'

'Agreed,' Sam said with a nod. Behind him, the door opened and Jay walked into the room.

'How you doing?' Jay asked with a smile.

'Not too bad,' Sam said. 'Considering what was supposed to happen to me.'

'Yeah, you look pretty good for a dead guy,' Jay said. 'He good to go, Doc?'

'Yes, Jacob, he appears to be well enough to meet everyone,' Stirling replied, 'and please don't call me that.'

'Sorry, Doc,' Jay said, 'force of habit. So, Sam, Rachel asked me to show you around. She's on the range at the moment, but she told me to tell you that she'd see you later. You ready?'

'I think so,' Sam said. 'Let's go.'

He followed Jay out into the corridor. It was as featureless as the room they'd just left, with the same grey, concrete walls and caged lights.

'So, you ready for the tour of our luxurious accommodations?' Jay asked as they walked.

'Sure,' Sam replied. 'What is this place anyway?'

'Closest thing we've got to home,' Jay said. 'The Doc brought us all here. Apparently we're underneath the place where he used to work. Don't know much about it, to be honest, just that it was some kind of government research laboratory. He doesn't talk about what he used to do.'

'How long have you been down here?' Sam asked as they walked past a door leading into a dormitory lined with bunk beds.

'Jackson found me about a year ago,' Jay said as

67

they reached a set of double doors at the end of the corridor.

'Jackson?'

'Yeah, he's the Doc's right-hand man. Taught us how to fight, proper bad ass. He used to be in the special forces—Royal Marine, I think. Do what he tells you and you'll both get along just fine.'

Jay pushed the doors open and led Sam into a much larger room beyond. There were just four people in the room, but Sam still hesitated. It might only have been four people, but that was four more people than he'd seen in the past eighteen months. He was still feeling overwhelmed by suddenly meeting all these new faces. Jay saw the look on Sam's face and smiled.

'It's OK,' he said, putting a hand on Sam's shoulder. 'I felt just the same when I first arrived. It was all a bit much to take in at first. I'd kinda got used to being on my own. You know what I mean?'

'Yeah,' Sam said quietly. 'I know exactly what you mean.'

On one side of the room there was a short dark-haired girl and a tall red-headed boy who were looking at a map on the wall and having what looked like quite a heated conversation. Sam followed as Jay walked towards them.

'Guys, I'd like to introduce you to our latest recruit,' Jay said. 'This is Sam. Sam, this is Kate and this is Adam—they're our resident scavengers.'

'I prefer the term *reclamation technician*, actually,' Adam said with a sniff.

'I dunno, I quite like the sound of scavenger,' Kate said, offering her hand to Sam. 'Makes us sound cooler.'

'Nice to meet you both,' Sam said, shaking

Kate's hand.

'If you need something, but you've got absolutely no idea where to find it, these two are the people who'll get it for you,' Jay explained.

'Assuming the Lost haven't got there before us, of course,' Adam said with a sigh.

'The Lost?' Sam asked.

'You know,' Kate said, 'everyone else. All the people who got wiped by the signal.'

'Oh, yeah right,' Sam said. 'I call them Walkers.'

'Walkers, Lost, whatever,' Adam said. 'The fact is that they're stripping the whole city bare. It's getting harder and harder to find the things we need. We're going to have to move further out of the city soon. Stirling knows it even if he doesn't want to admit it.'

'OK, Adam,' Kate said, shaking her head slightly, 'don't lecture the new guy. Everyone's already heard what you think, but you know it's not as simple as that. Not all of us can just leave.'

'I wasn't saying that we should all . . .' Adam began.

'OK, OK, enough,' Jay said, holding his hands up. 'Much as I would love to have this conversation *again*, I was actually hoping to introduce Sam to everyone else at some point today.'

'Fine, whatever,' Adam said, turning back to the map on the wall. 'No one ever listens to me anyway.'

'That's not true,' Kate said. 'I listen to you. How else would I be able to tell you exactly why you're wrong?'

'Come on,' Jay said, nodding his head towards the three battered old sofas arranged in a U-shape in the middle of the room where two girls were sitting chatting while another boy was reading a book.

'OK, Sam,' Jay said, pointing to each of the others in turn, 'this is Liz, Nat and Toby.'

'Hi,' the boy called Toby said, lowering his book. 'Welcome to our burrow.'

'Toby runs the kitchen,' Jay explained. 'He's the one who makes sure we all get fed.'

'Only because if I let anyone else do it we'd all be dead of food poisoning within a week,' Toby said with a crooked smile before retreating behind his book again.

'So, Sam, tell us, is it true what Rachel said?' Nat asked. 'Did you really get stung by a Hunter?'

'Um . . . yeah, I suppose I did,' Sam said, sounding slightly uncomfortable.

'Got to tell you, then,' the girl called Liz said, 'you're a whole lot more alive than you should be.'

'Yeah, that's what everyone keeps telling me,' Sam said with a sheepish grin. 'I'm just lucky, I suppose.'

'You can say that again,' Nat said, shaking her head slightly.

'Nat's a surface operative like me and Rach,' Jay explained, 'and Liz is in charge of the stores.'

'So, you'd better be nice to me if you ever want anything,' Liz added.

'Yeah, but don't forget that's the *only* reason anyone's nice to you,' Nat said with a smile.

'Anyway, much as we'd love to stay and chat all day,' Jay said, 'we're on our way to see Jackson and you know how he hates to be kept waiting.'

'Ooooh, you don't want to make Jackson angry,' Liz said, shaking her head. 'You wouldn't like him when he's angry.'

'I'll tell him you said that, shall I?' Jay asked.

'Actually, no, probably I'd rather you didn't,' Liz said.

'Thought not,' Jay said. 'Come on, Sam.'

Jay led him out of the room and along another corridor.

'Dining area and the storerooms are down there,' he said, pointing to a corridor that branched off to the left. They continued, passing a couple more closed doors. 'Those are the Doc's and Jackson's rooms,' he added as they walked past. They continued walking and soon reached a T-junction at the end of the corridor where they headed left, towards another set of double doors. 'And in here,' he concluded, pushing the doors open, 'are the labs.'

Jay walked down the room past the benches covered in scientific equipment to the far end where Will and a tall girl with long blonde hair tied back in a ponytail were both staring at an LCD monitor.

'I still don't get it,' Will said as Sam and Jay approached. 'I mean, I understand the basics, but I don't see how Stirling isolated the waveform in the first place without ...'

'Sorry to break up brainiac club, Will,' Jay said, 'but I wanted to introduce Sam to Anne.'

'Oh, hi, Jay, Sam, of course. Sorry, I was just trying to get my head around this training exercise,' Will said, pushing his glasses back up his nose. 'Anne, this is our walking miracle. The one I was telling you about.'

'Hi, pleased to meet you, Sam,' said Anne. 'Will told me about what happened to you. I suppose you know by now how lucky you are to be alive.'

71

'Yeah,' Sam said, 'so everybody keeps telling me.'

'I'm sorry, you must be sick of hearing it,' Anne said. 'It's just that we've all seen what normally happens to someone who gets stung and . . . well . . . it's not good.'

'Stirling's locked away in his lab trying to work out how you survived,' Will said. 'I'm not sure I've ever seen him this puzzled before.'

'Well, it's nice to know that I've now officially been elevated to the status of scientific curiosity,' Sam said, raising an eyebrow at Jay.

'Yup, I suppose I'd better get you out of here before these two start sticking needles in you as well,' Jay replied with a nod.

'Actually,' Anne said, smiling, 'a full autopsy might be more efficient.'

'OK, creeping me out now,' Sam said.

'Don't worry, she gets less creepy once you get to know her properly,' Jay said. 'But only slightly.'

'Anyway, nice to meet you, Sam,' Anne said. 'I hope that you've not been given too bad an impression of us by being shown around by this idiot.'

She and Will turned their attention back to the diagram on the screen as Jay and Sam headed out of the lab.

'That was some pretty impressive-looking kit in there,' Sam said. 'Where did it all come from?'

'Adam and Kate found some of it, but most of it was brought down from the building above us,' Jay said, pointing up towards the ceiling. 'It was nearly all set up by the time I came here. Stirling had already been training Will and Anne for months; he's always saying that we can only win through

72

science, or something like that. Gotta admit that pretty much all of what he's got them working on and studying just goes straight over my head. I guess that's why I'm on the surface-ops team. Best place to be if you ask me, though. I think I'd go crazy if I was stuck down here all the time.'

They walked down the corridor in silence.

'I've been wondering how this place is powered,' Sam asked, pointing at one of the lights in the ceiling. 'The power everywhere else went out about a week after *they* turned up.'

'You mean the aliens?' Jay asked, looking him in the eye.

'Well, it might sound sort of stupid, but that's what I've always thought they must be,' Sam said.

'Yeah, me too,' Jay said with a nod. 'Stirling always says that "their origins are unclear", but I say if it looks like an alien and it acts like an alien, then it pretty much has to be an alien. If you want to know what to call them round here, though, Stirling calls them the Threat and now that name's pretty much stuck.'

'The Threat,' Sam said. 'Yeah, that sounds about right.'

'As for how the whole place is powered, apparently it's thanks to a generator in the building up top. Believe it or not, we've got our own little nuclear reactor just like the ones they put on submarines. Least that's what Stirling tells us.'

'What was this place before the Threat arrived?' Sam asked with a frown. 'I know you said it was a government facility, but a nuclear reactor in the middle of London? What were they doing up there?'

'No idea,' Jay said, shaking his head. 'You can

try asking Stirling himself if you want, but you'll just get the same answer that we always do—that it's none of our business.'

'That's all he's ever told you? Don't you think he owes you more than that?'

'I don't think the Doc thinks he owes anyone anything,' Jay said with a shrug. 'He's not forcing any of us to stay here, but it's not like there's anywhere better to go. I mean, sure, we've all got our theories about Stirling and this place, but don't hold your breath waiting for any more than that. You're not going to get any answers from him or Jackson.'

Sam thought about what Jay had just told him. There was something weird about Stirling's refusal to give any more detail about what this place was and why it seemed to be so carefully prepared for such an unlikely scenario.

'So, tell me, how'd you survive up there for so long on your own?' Jay asked as they headed through another door and started down another flight of stairs leading to a lower level.

'I didn't,' Sam said.'Survive *up there*, I mean. I spent nearly all my time hiding in the sewers. I only went to the surface during the night and even then I tried to keep my time above ground to a minimum. You know what it's like with the Drones . . . I mean, what do you call them . . . erm . . . the Hunters buzzing around up there.'

'Yeah, I do,' Jay said, a sudden look of sadness flashing across his face. 'I'm not sure that this is really what people meant when they talked about an *underground* resistance movement.'

'Probably not,' Sam said, following him down the stairs, 'but at least you guys are resisting. I was just

74

hiding.'

'Hey, we were all hiding till Stirling found us,' Jay said with a shrug. 'That's probably why we're still alive.'

'I suppose,' Sam replied. 'So, Stirling found all of you?'

'Yeah, far as I know,' Jay replied. 'Every so often he'll send us out looking for a "contact" in a certain area and nine times out of ten we end up finding someone wandering around, just like you were.'

'So how does he know where to look?' Sam asked.

'No idea,' Jay said, shaking his head. 'I don't know how he finds us. I've asked him, we all have, but you can probably guess by now what his answer always is.'

'Let me guess,' Sam said. 'It's none of our business.'

'Yeah,' Jay replied, 'like I said, the Doc's not big on explanations. Sure, it's frustrating sometimes, but no one's forcing us to stay here. His house, his rules.'

Sam nodded, but he still wanted to know more about Stirling and the facility that seemed to have become his new home. All the evidence pointed to the fact that Stirling knew far more about the invaders than he was letting on. Jay might have given up asking why that was, but he needed some more concrete answers before he could be sure that Stirling was someone he should trust.

'Can I ask you something else?' Sam said after a few moments' silence.

'Sure,' Jay replied.

'I was just thinking about something that Rachel said when I first met her,' Sam said with a slight

75

frown. 'She told me that you'd been looking for me for a long time.'Do you know what she meant?'

'Yeah,' Jay said. 'Stirling had sent us up top seven or eight times over the past couple of months looking for someone, but we never found any sign of anybody in the target area. It was weird because it never usually took us that long to track down whoever the Doc had sent us to find.'

'Hey, don't worry about it,' Sam said. 'Over the past eighteen months I've got really, *really* good at hiding.'

'Haven't we all?'

They reached the bottom of the last flight of stairs and headed through the fire door. Sam flinched involuntarily at the sudden sound of gunfire. It was a sound that he'd only really heard on television or at the cinema up until a couple of days ago and he still couldn't get over just how *loud* it was. The room they had entered was long with a high ceiling held up by thick concrete pillars. Dotted around the room were tables that were covered in tactical equipment of all kinds; night-vision goggles, field dressing kits: ration packs, maps, backpacks, body armour, everything that a well-equipped soldier might need.

'Home sweet home,' Jay said, 'or to give it its proper name, the Operations Training Area. This is where we learn how to take the fight to the Threat. You see that guy down there by the range? That's Jackson.'

Further down the room there was a shooting range constructed out of sandbags where Sam could see Rachel and another boy standing with pistols raised, aiming at paper targets. Standing behind them was a muscular man who looked to be in his late thirties or early forties wearing a black T-shirt and grey, camouflage-patterned trousers tucked into combat boots. His head was shaved and his cold grey eyes watched carefully as Rachel and the boy fired at their targets.

'Trust me when I say that, apart from the Doc, Jackson is the one person in this place you really don't want to mess,' Jay said. 'I'll introduce you to him in a minute, but first I want you to meet someone else. Come on.'

Jay walked over to a heavy steel door set into the wall with a skull and crossbones hand-painted on it.

'This is the armoury,' Jay said as he opened the door, 'where we keep all the really cool toys.'

Sam followed Jay inside and let out a low whistle.

'OK, that's a lot of guns.'

The room was divided in two by a long counter, behind which the walls were lined with racks and shelving, filled with a breathtaking array of different weapons. There were pistols, assault rifles, shotguns, rocket launchers and grenades, as well as numerous crates of ammunition. Sam reckoned that it looked like just about everything someone would need to fight a small war—or a *big* war for that matter. Sitting with his feet up on the countertop, reading a comic book, was a boy with bright red dyed hair, wearing jeans, flip-flops and a T-shirt with the words 'From My Cold, Dead Hands' on it. He looked up as Jay and Sam walked in and smiled.

'Jay, how you doing, man?' the boy asked.

'I'm good,' Jay said as he bumped fists with the other boy. 'Just wanted to introduce you to the latest stray we found wandering the streets.'

'That would be me,' Sam said.

'Sam, this is Jack,' Jay said, jerking a thumb towards the boy behind the counter. 'He's pretty much certifiable, but he knows a lot about guns.'

'Hey,' Jack said, 'you're the one who goes up top and gets chased by homicidal aliens and you call me crazy? So, Sam, you going to the surface with these nutters or is Stirling going to have you washing test tubes?'

'Umm . . . I don't really know yet,' Sam said.

'Rach says he can handle himself,' Jay said, 'so I reckon he'll be coming out with us.'

'Sounds to me like Jay thinks you're going to be one of my regular customers,' Jack said, raising an eyebrow. 'Sorry about that.'

'Hey, it's better than being stuck in a hole underground,' Jay retorted.

'Yeah, you know what, you're right, there's nothing worse than a nice, safe, warm hole underground,' Jack said, nodding.

'Where did you get all this stuff?' Sam asked, looking around the room.

'Oh, we've been collecting for a while,' Jack said. 'Jackson always seems to know where to find the best kit. You actually met the big man yet?'

'No, I wanted him to meet you first,' Jay said. 'Thought I'd save the best till last.'

'Just remember when you meet him, Sam, that his bark is worse than his bite,' Jack said. 'Actually, no, now I come to think of it, his bite's just as bad. Never mind, I'm sure you're going to love him.'

'Are you going to be watching the movie later?' Jay asked.

'So what's Liz got for us to watch tonight?' Jack asked.

78

'Oh, just a little something that Adam found on a scouting mission last week,' Jay said with a smile.

'Come on, don't tease me,' Jack said. 'What is it?'

'*Die Hard*,' Jay replied with a grin.

'Oh, I am so there,' Jack said, grinning back.

'OK, we'll see you in the common room later,' Jay said.

'Later, guys,' Jack said with a wave, picking up his comic book.

Sam followed Jay out of the armoury and across the Ops Area towards the firing range. Rachel and the other boy had finished shooting and Jackson was watching as they carefully field stripped and cleaned their weapons. Sam was impressed by the speed with which they disassembled the pistols and set about cleaning the component parts. When he had realised that there were other survivors fighting back against the Threat, he had expected to find a ragtag bunch of kids with guns, but what he saw around him was a well-trained and disciplined guerilla force. That had to be down to this man called Jackson. He looked every inch the professional soldier and, if what Jay had already told him was true, he was the one responsible for turning a bunch of frightened kids into something resembling the beginnings of an army. He looked up as Jay and Sam approached.

'Good morning, Jacob,' Jackson said. 'I assume that this is our new recruit.'

'Yeah,' Jay replied. 'I've just been giving him the guided tour.'

'Robert Jackson. Pleased to meet you,' he said, offering Sam his hand.

'Sam Riley,' Sam said, shaking his hand. 'Pleased

to meet you too.'

'You've met Rachel, of course,' Jackson said, 'and this is Tim, another member of the Ops Team.'

'Hi, Sam,' Tim said as he pushed a brush through the barrel of his dismantled pistol. 'Hope Jay hasn't been annoying you too much.'

'Rachel tells me that you put up a good fight when you encountered the Threat forces on the surface,' Jackson said. 'What's even more impressive is that you did it while suffering the effects of a Hunter sting. How are you feeling now—fully recovered?'

'Yes, I think so,' Sam replied. He glanced over at Rachel who smiled back at him.

'Good,' Jackson said. 'I understand what you've been through, Sam. I know that you've spent the past year and a half running, hiding, struggling just to survive, but we're going to teach you to do more than that; we're going to teach you how to fight.'

Sam thought of the world, the people he'd lost and he suddenly felt something cold and hard in the pit of his stomach.

'You know, I think I'd like that,' Sam said with a nod. 'I think I'd like that a lot.'

'Excellent,' Jackson said, gesturing to a pistol on one of the tables nearby. 'Then we might as well get started right now.'

A couple of hours later Sam was sitting with the others eating lunch. He hadn't really realised how hungry he actually was until Toby had handed him the steaming bowl of vegetable chilli and rice that he was now devouring. The other kids he'd met over the past couple of hours were chatting and laughing as they ate. Sam ate in silence, partly because he was enjoying a proper hot cooked meal for the first time in a very long time, but also because he was simply enjoying listening to the bubbling sound of the conversation around him. It was funny how something that he would have once taken for granted could have now become so special.

'Looks like you're enjoying that,' Rachel said with a smile as she sat down opposite him.

'You have no idea,' Sam said with a sigh.

'I think you impressed Jackson on the range this morning,' she said, 'and trust me when I say that he is *not* an easy man to please.'

'Yeah, I kind of got that impression actually,' Sam said, raising an eyebrow. 'How long have you been training with him?'

'Since I first got here and that was only a couple of months after the Threat landed, so I suppose that must be getting on for a year and a half now.'

'So were you one of the first people that they found?' Sam asked.

'Yeah, though Jack and Will were here before me.'

'So how did they find you?'

'I don't really know, to be honest,' Rachel said, shaking her head slightly. 'After the Signal I was hiding in the back offices of a superstore. I only ventured out to grab what I needed off the shelves. Then one day Jackson and Redmond were waiting for me out in the store. I almost had a heart attack when I saw them. I thought they were a couple of the Lost at first. You know, people wiped by the Signal . . .'

'Walkers.'

'Yeah, then Redmond says, "Hello there" and I freaked out. I ran, but they caught up with me and explained that they weren't going to hurt me, just take me somewhere safe. I was so glad to see other people who'd not had their brains wiped. Then they brought me back here.'

'Who's Redmond?' Sam asked. 'I don't think I've met him yet.'

'Yeah, well, you won't,' Rachel said, her eyes suddenly dropping to look at the table. 'He and Jackson were really close. I got the impression that they'd served together for a while. Then, one day, about six months ago, they both went up to the surface on a retrieval op, but only Jackson came back.'

'I'm sorry,' Sam said.

'Don't worry about it,' Rachel said with a sigh. 'He's not the first person we've lost and I doubt he'll be the last. Nobody really knows what happened up there, but I'll tell you this much; Jackson's not been back to the surface since.'

'He doesn't strike me as the sort of person who scares easily,' Sam said.

'He's not,' Rachel replied. 'That's what worries everyone.'

They both ate in silence for a few seconds and Sam looked around the table at the others.

'So, how come there's no one else here who's older than us?' Sam asked. 'Surely Stirling and Jackson can't be the only people over fifteen years old that weren't affected by the Signal?'

'I wish I knew,' Rachel said. 'The only people

we've ever been sent out to find were about the same age as us. I asked Stirling about it once and he told me that it probably had something to do with the fact that our brains were still developing and that somehow that made us immune to whatever it was that the Threat did to everyone else, but I'm not sure he was telling me everything. That's not all that unusual, though. You'll find that Stirling likes to play his cards pretty close to his chest.'

'Yeah, so I keep hearing. Jay told me that he always seems to know where to go to find people who weren't wiped by the signal, and that was how you found me.'

'Yeah, that's right,' Rachel nodded, 'but before we found you we hadn't met anyone else who'd not been brainwashed by the Signal for a couple of months. We're all worried that there might not be many more of us out there. Or worse, that there might not be *any* more of us.'

'There's got to be more people who weren't affected,' Sam said. 'Just think, if you've found this many people already, then there have to be more. It's a big planet.'

'Sure, but what good does it do us if there are people like us in America or Australia? We've got no way of communicating with them, no way of organising any sort of concerted resistance to the Threat.'

'So what do you suggest? Should we just hide and hope that eventually they go away?'

'I'm not saying that,' Rachel said, frowning, 'but we do need hope. It's not enough that we just survive—we need to fight back.'

'Isn't that what we're being trained to do?' Sam

asked.

'Of course it is,' Rachel replied, 'but I do wonder sometimes if we can really make a difference?'

'Well, four days ago I thought I was the last person on the planet who had free will,' Sam said, looking her in the eye. 'I was convinced that I was going to spend the rest of my life running and hiding. Now, in the space of just a few days, I feel like there's hope again and that maybe we can fight these things. And do you know why I feel that way? Well, it's because, no matter what happens, I'm not alone any more. None of us are.'

Rachel stopped eating and looked up for a few seconds.

'Maybe you're right,' she said finally, smiling at him.

'Right about what?' Jay asked as he sat down next to them.

'I was just saying that I think that this might be the best chilli I've ever tasted,' Sam said with a grin.

'Yeah, it's all right, I suppose. It could do with some meat in it, though,' Jay said.

'Here we go,' Rachel said, rolling her eyes.

'What? It's not fair. No matter how many times I ask the Doc, he still won't let me try to find some cows to bring down here.'

'The sad thing is, he's not actually joking,' Rachel said to Sam. 'He really has asked.'

'The Doc's always going on about dangerous levels of methane build-up in a confined space, but just ask yourself this, if he's really so worried about that, why are we all eating vegetarian chilli?'

And then Sam did something he hadn't done for a very long time. He laughed.

6

The next couple of months seemed to pass by in a blur for Sam. At times it felt like his feet had barely touched the ground since he had woken up in the infirmary. Stirling had explained to him early on that every one of them was expected to be useful to the group in some way. It had been clear pretty much from the start that he wasn't going to be joining Will and Anne in the lab, but there was no way he was going to just help out around the base in some logistical capacity either. He knew exactly where he wanted to be—on the surface Ops Team, and that was exactly where he'd ended up.

The training schedule that Jackson had put together for him had been punishing and relentless, both mentally and physically. He had learned not only how to fight but also *when* to fight. Jackson spent as much time teaching the Ops Team about the theory of guerilla warfare as he did showing them how to shoot.

'The most powerful weapon you have is the one inside your skull,' was what he told them over and over again. They had no chance of winning a stand-up fight against the Threat so they had to fight smart and they had to fight dirty, hitting the enemy and then fading away before they had a chance to retaliate.

The physical training had been exhausting, with workout sessions that were so regular that after a while they all seemed to blur into one. At the same time he was being taught not just how to shoot, but how to field-strip and clean his weapon, or how to plant explosives, or how to make the best use of cover. He had kept asking both Jackson and Stirling for more details about the facility and their knowledge of the Threat, but just as Jay had warned, his questions remained unanswered. He could sense that the others were equally frustrated by this lack of information, but there really was nothing they could do about it. No one was forcing him to stay, as he had been reminded on more than one occasion, but that didn't change the fact that he was determined to get some answers to the questions buzzing around inside his head.

Now, as Sam stood, assault rifle raised, aiming at the target at the far end of the range, he realised that he was actually starting to feel less like a frightened survivor and more like a soldier, and he had to admit that it felt good. He gently squeezed the trigger and put a three-round burst of fire into the centre of the target.

'Good,' Jackson said, 'but, remember, don't anticipate the trigger point; a good marksman is always slightly surprised when their weapon discharges.'

Sam gave a quick nod and fired again, putting another burst into the centre of the target.

'OK, let's see how you do against moving targets,' Jackson said, nodding towards a door on the other side of the Ops Training Area. Sam placed the rifle on the rack next to the range and followed Jackson across the room. Rachel and Nat were already waiting for them, both checking their weapons.

'I see you've returned for a little more ritual humiliation,' Nat said with a smile as Sam approached. 'Talk about being a sucker for punishment.'

'You got lucky last time,' Sam said as he picked his own pistol up. He took one of the small gas canisters from the box on the table and screwed it into the bottom of the grip. The paintball gun felt light in his hand in comparison to the real thing, but for live fire training purposes it was their only real option.

'OK, enough chatter,' Jackson said with a slight frown. 'Rachel and Natalie, you have three minutes before I send Sam in. I trust you'll make it as difficult as possible for him.'

'Oh, don't worry about that,' Rachel said. 'I give him thirty seconds tops from the moment he walks through the door.'

'Be surprised if he makes it that long,' Nat said as they both entered the training area.

'OK,' Jackson said to Sam as the door closed behind the girls, 'you're facing an entrenched enemy that knows you're coming. What's their greatest weakness?'

'Overconfidence,' Sam replied.

'Correct,' Jackson said. 'Which is something that you can take advantage of. Now, remember what I told you the other day about the secret to fighting an enemy with superior forces? What did Sun Tzu say?'

'"If you have a superior force, make for easy ground; with an inferior one, make for difficult ground",' Sam replied.

'Good,' Jackson said. 'So get in there and make them fight on your terms. Find the difficult ground.'

Sam thought about Jackson's advice for a couple of minutes and then an idea suddenly occurred to him.

'OK, ready?' Jackson asked a few seconds later, looking at his watch.

'Ready,' Sam replied.

'Go,' Jackson said, pushing open the door to the training room.

Jackson watched Sam enter the training room and then turned towards a narrow staircase leading to a dimly lit room. At one end of the room was a large one-way mirrored window that allowed him to observe Rachel and Nat as they made their way carefully through the maze of training rooms below. The dummy walls were only made of plywood and they had no ceilings, but they were useful for training the Ops Team how to fight in enclosed urban spaces. Jackson heard the sound of footsteps on the stairs behind him and he turned to see Stirling enter the room.

'Morning, Iain,' Jackson said. 'Don't see you up here very often.'

'Yes, I know, but I've located a possible target of opportunity and I wanted to discuss putting an Ops mission together to go and have a look at it.'

'No problem,' Jackson replied. 'Just let me watch this exercise and then we can talk about it.'

Stirling came up and stood alongside Jackson and looked down at the training area.

'Who's in there?' Stirling asked.

'It's Rachel and Nat versus Sam,' Jackson said, watching as the two girls advanced through another area, covering each other's backs, in a textbook room-clearing sweep.

'That seems somewhat unfair,' Stirling said.

'They have to learn how to fight when outnumbered,' Jackson said, 'because they always

88

will be on the surface.'

'True,' Stirling said. 'Where is Samuel?'

'I'm not sure,' Jackson said. He couldn't see Sam anywhere within the training course.

Suddenly, a purple paintball hit Nat squarely between the shoulder blades, and she reluctantly lowered her weapon and knelt on the floor to show she was out of action. Rachel whirled round and another paintball hit her in the chest. Jackson was still trying to work out where Sam was when a slight movement on top of the lighting rig that illuminated the training course caught his eye. Sam was lying flat on top of the metal frame, with his gun pointing down at the girls below.

'Clever lad, you found the difficult ground,' Jackson said. 'Well done.'

'Is that allowed?' Stirling asked, raising an eyebrow.

'No, but that's why I like him. He's a good shot and he's bright. Not only that, he's a born leader. Which is exactly what we need right now. He's ready to go back up top.'

'Good, because, as I mentioned, I have a job for your team,' Stirling said.

'Right, I'll come and find you,' Jackson said, following Stirling down the stairs.

Stirling headed out of the Ops Training Area and back to the upper level as Jackson approached Sam, Nat and Rachel who were having a heated conversation.

'You cheated,' Nat said, jabbing her finger into Sam's chest as he grinned back at her.

'There's no such thing as cheating,' Jackson said. 'There's alive and there's dead. You were thinking two-dimensionally. Don't get horizon focused—

an enemy can attack from above or below. Sam, good job. Get cleaned up and then go and get some lunch.'

'We have located a new alien transmission source,' Stirling said, looking at the five members of the Ops Team in front of him. Sam, Jay, Tim, Nat and Rachel listened as Stirling began the briefing with Jackson beside him.

'The signal from that source is extremely unusual,' Stirling said, 'and extremely worrying. The reason it is of such concern is that up until now the only Threat transmission source with this kind of power was the main Threat vessel hovering above central London. What I need you to do is find whatever is transmitting this new signal and, if possible, destroy it. We must do everything we can to slow the spread of the Threat's influence and this may well be a perfect opportunity to do just that.'

'So we have no idea what this thing actually is?' Rachel asked.

'No, not really,' Jackson replied. 'Adam and Kate did try to scout the location, but they couldn't get inside the stadium.'

'The stadium?' Jay said. 'Where is this thing?'

'Right here,' Jackson said, pointing at a location on the large map of London that covered the wall.

'Great,' Jay said with a grin. 'I've always wanted to play Wembley.'

'How heavily guarded is it?' Tim asked.

'Outside it's not too bad,' Jackson replied. 'Kate

90

and Adam saw Hunter patrols, but nothing worse than that. Inside, we just don't know.'

'How much do you want to bet that, whatever this thing is, it's got a Grendel sitting on top of it,' Rachel said.

'It's a possibility,' Jackson said. 'I don't like to send you in blind like this, so no heroics. Get in, plant charges on this thing if you can and get out. If it's too well protected, pull out and we'll try a different approach. OK?'

'When do we head out?' Jay asked.

'Three hours from now,' Jackson replied. 'You've got until then for equipment and weapons prep and tactical breakdowns. So I suggest we get started.'

Jay carefully pushed the steel hatch open just a few centimetres and peered outside. After scanning the surroundings he turned to the others and gave a single quick nod before heading out. The others followed him into the enclosed courtyard, all feeling the sudden chill of the cold night air. Jay raised his rifle to his shoulder, sighting down the barrel and moved quickly across the courtyard towards the archway leading to the street. They stopped, backs pressed against the archway wall as Jay quickly peeked his head round the corner, checking for any sign of Threat activity. He headed down the street with the others close behind, all moving towards their target as silently as possible.

They arrived at the end of the broad pedestrianised street that led to the entrance of the enormous stadium half a mile away. Overhead, the moon disappeared behind a cloud bank and the street was plunged into shadow. The Ops Team activated their night-vision goggles and proceeded cautiously down the concourse, moving between cover positions quickly and efficiently, just as they had been trained to do. Jay suddenly held up his arm, fist clenched; the silent signal to hold position. A moment later they heard the familiar sound of approaching Hunters. Sam scanned the surroundings, all bathed in the eerie green glow of the night-vision goggles. He spotted a pair of Hunters gliding across the street less than a hundred metres away. He held his breath, watching as they floated out of sight, seemingly oblivious to the team's presence.

'OK, guys,' Jay's voice whispered in his earpiece, 'stay sharp, keep your eyes and ears wide open. We don't want any nasty surprises.'

Jay slid out from behind the fast-food kiosk where he'd been taking cover and continued along the street with the rest of the team close behind. The darkened stadium loomed over them and Sam began to feel the nervous fluttering of butterflies in his stomach. It didn't matter how intensively he had trained for this, it didn't quiet the voice in the back of his head telling him that he was walking straight into the lion's den. He followed as Jay led the way up the long ramp to the stadium entrance, eager to avoid staying out in the open any longer. Sam had expected there to be more patrols, but there was no sign of any Hunters as they approached the top of the ramp. For some reason, that just made him more nervous.

One of the automated turnstiles that once would

have checked people's tickets stood wide open and the five of them passed through one by one and into the vaulted concourse that encircled the stadium.

'Oh God,' Nat's voice whispered in Sam's ear as they took in the sight that greeted them. The floor of the concourse was filled, as far as the eye could see, with people lying in neatly ordered rows, flat on their backs with their eyes shut. Sam's mind flashed back to the first night after the arrival of the Threat and the warehouse that was just the same. Suddenly, he saw his sister's face in his mind, looking just as it had on that night, the last time he had ever seen her.

He shook his head and told himself to focus.

'OK,' Rachel said quietly, 'we all know that there's nothing we can do for them now. We need to keep moving.'

Jay pulled the handset that Stirling had given him from one of the pouches on his chest and examined the display.

'OK, on me,' he said, setting off across the concourse.

They picked their way carefully between the rows of bodies, following Jay as he studied the direction and range indicator, hunting for the source of the transmissions that Stirling had intercepted.

'Have you seen this before?' Sam asked Rachel, gesturing at the dormant bodies that lined the concourse floor.

'A couple of times,' Rachel said with a frown. 'This is how the Threat store people who were wiped by the Signal. It's always large buildings like this—kind of mass dormitories, I suppose. Creepy

93

as hell, no matter how many times you see it.'

'You can say that again,' Sam said.

'The source seems to be inside the stadium itself,' Jay said, looking up from the scanner and over to one of the numerous gates that led into the central arena.

'Can I just go on record as saying that this feels all wrong,' Nat said, looking both ways down the concourse, her rifle raised. 'If this thing is as important as Stirling thinks it is, why isn't it better protected? This is too easy.'

'Maybe the Threat weren't expecting any kind of attack,' Rachel said. 'Perhaps they're just assuming that they don't *need* to protect the transmitter.'

'Hey, I'm not complaining,' Jay said. 'I kinda like easy. Come on.'

The others followed as Jay headed through the archway and into the stadium. Sam's mouth dropped open in amazement as he looked around. The stadium was filled to capacity, every seat taken by dormant Walkers. There was no sound except for the creepy whisper of tens of thousands of people breathing. Below them in the centre of the green rectangle of overgrown grass that had once been the most famous football pitch in England was a black spire, twenty metres high, made up of dozens of huge, angular obsidian shards. Occasional pulses of green light shot across the surface of the spire, sending ripples of light dancing across the grass.

'I'm guessing that might just be what we're looking for,' Sam said quietly.

'You know, I think you might be right,' Jay replied.

The five of them walked down the stairs

between the sections of banked seating, heading towards the pitch. As they got closer, Sam began to hear a muted, throbbing hum that seemed to be emanating from the transmission spire. The sound was deeply unpleasant, resonating inside his skull and filling his head with a dull ache.

'What is that?' Sam asked, rubbing his temples as the sound grew louder and louder the nearer they got to the spire.

'What is what?' Rachel asked, looking slightly confused.

'That sound,' Sam said. 'It's giving me a headache.'

'What sound?' Nat asked, frowning. 'I can't hear anything.'

'It's coming from that thing,' Sam said, pointing at the black monolith. 'I can't believe you can't hear it.'

'I don't hear anything either,' Jay said, turning and looking at Sam. 'Are you sure you're feeling OK?'

'Yeah, I'm fine. Let's just plant the charges so we can get out of here,' Sam said, backing away from the Threat transmitter. He took another few steps away from the spire and realised with growing unease that the sound wasn't getting quieter as he moved further from it; in fact, it was getting louder. Now he could hear another sound within the subsonic thrum: a high-pitched whispering noise that felt like it was scratching at the inside of his skull. He gradually realised that he could make out something bizarre within this hissing sound, something that sounded almost like *voices*. He couldn't make out what the voices were saying, but it definitely sounded like some sort of language.

95

Sam tried to ignore the sound and focus on the rest of the team, watching as Jay placed the explosive charge on the base of the spire.

'OK,' Jay said, 'once I hit the switch we've got five minutes to get clear before these puppies blow.'

'What about all these people?' Nat asked.

'The blast radius shouldn't be more than about ten metres,' Jay said. 'They'll be fine.'

Jay hit the switch on the timer and Sam yelped in pain as the whisper in his head turned into a scream. Suddenly he heard what sounded like a multitude of answering screams that seemed to come from somewhere above them.

'We need to get out of here now,' Sam said as he looked upwards.

'Don't worry,' Jay said. 'We've got five minutes —that's more than enough time to get clear.'

'It's not the explosion I'm worried about,' Sam said, pointing up towards the stadium roof.

The others looked where Sam was pointing and realised exactly what he was talking about. The entire underside of the stadium's domed roof was covered in Hunters, countless thousands of them hanging upside down from the ceiling.

'Oh my God,' Rachel said as the first of the alien creatures began to detach themselves from their perches and drop towards them. 'It's a nest.'

'RUN!' Jay yelled at the top of his voice when the trickle of Hunters dropping towards them quickly turned into a torrent as the alarm spread throughout the swarm. The buzzing drone from the ever-swelling host of Hunters grew louder and louder as Sam and the others sprinted across the grass towards the nearest flight of stairs that led

96

out of the arena. The five of them bounded up the stairs, taking them two or three at a time. As they ran through the archway and on to the outer concourse, Tim turned and raised his rifle, opening fire at the nearest Hunters, the hammering noise of his rifle echoing off the concrete walls.

'Tim!' Jay bellowed as Sam and the girls ran on ahead. 'Don't be stupid! We've got to get out of here now. There's no way we can fight that many of them.'

Tim fired one last burst into the mass of silver creatures before running after Jay. Sam pointed at another block of automated turnstiles set into the outside wall fifty metres away.

'Come on,' he yelled. 'That's our way out.'

They sprinted between the dormant Walkers covering the floor around them, and headed for the exit, the deafening buzz from the pursuing Hunters filling the air. Sam felt a sudden moment of despair as he realised that the gates ahead of them, unlike the ones they'd entered through, were firmly sealed.

'There's no way out here,' Nat shouted. 'Keep moving. Head for the next gate!'

Tim turned and fired another burst into the swirling mass of Hunters just thirty metres behind them and getting closer all the time. It was pointless; he might as well have been shooting at a tidal wave.

'Oh no,' Nat said under her breath, coming to a standstill.

Sam ran up beside her and stopped as he saw what she had seen. The concourse ahead of them was filled with Hunters coming in the opposite direction. They were cut off from the exit. Sam looked around desperately, trying to spot some way for them to escape. 'Everyone! This way!' He hopped over the unconscious bodies and vaulted across one of the refreshment counters that were set into the outside wall of the concourse, with Rachel and Nat just behind him. Jay and Tim stood back to back, firing at the waves of Hunters that were now advancing on them from both directions.

'Help me!' Sam yelled at the two girls as he climbed up on to the counter and grabbed the bottom edge of the rolling steel security shutter protruding from the ceiling above them. The three of them pulled as hard as they could and the shutter began to slowly inch downwards.

'Jay! Tim!' Sam shouted. 'Come on!'

Jay lowered his rifle and sprinted towards the counter, sliding over it and then grabbing the shutter and pulling on it as hard as he could. Tim backed towards the counter, still firing at the nearest Hunters who were getting closer all the time.

'Tim, get in here!' Jay yelled. 'Now!'

Tim stopped firing, turned and ran towards them. He was only five metres away when he tripped over the legs of one of the brainwashed people lying on the floor. He fell forward, landing flat on top of another dormant Walker. He tried to scramble back to his feet, but it was too late. He barely had time to scream as the Hunters hit him from both sides, and he disappeared in a whirling mass of stinging tentacles.

'NO!' Jay screamed. He was halfway back over the counter before Sam caught hold of his pack and dragged him back inside.

'There's nothing you can do. He's gone,' Sam

shouted, grabbing the bottom of the shutter again and hauling it downwards with all his might. Jay hesitated, just for a second, and then he too helped them finally slam the shutter down on to the counter. Sam quickly threw the bolt at the bottom, locking it firmly in place. Moments later the shutter began to rattle and bang as the Hunters on the other side attacked it. Jay, Sam and Rachel leant against the shutter trying to brace it against the onslaught.

'Nat, we need a way out!' Rachel said.

Nat dashed into the back of the store, looking around desperately for an exit. She spotted a door at the far end of the room and carefully opened it, wary of what might be waiting on the other side. The room was lined with shelves filled with cardboard boxes that had once contained food for the hungry visitors to the stadium. Their contents had long since rotted and now the boxes were covered in mould. Nat walked to the back of the storeroom, and felt her heart sink as she realised that there was no obvious way out. She ran back to the others who were still desperately trying to support the steel shutters against the ferocious, relentless assault from the other side.

'There's nothing back there,' Nat said, fighting to keep any sign of the panic she was starting to feel out of her voice.

'There's got to be a way out,' Sam said with a grunt as something slammed into the shutter right next to him.

'There is,' Nat said, pointing at the security door next to the counter that led back out into the concourse.

'Well, we're not going that way,' Jay said. 'Please

don't tell me that's the only way out of here.'

'It's not,' Sam said, as he suddenly realised what they were going to have to do. He leapt down off the counter and ran over to Jay. 'Give me your pack.'

'What are you going to do?' Jay asked, frowning, shrugging off his backpack and handing it to Sam.

'I'm going to get us out of here,' Sam replied, running towards the storeroom.

Jay turned back to the shutter just as a Hunter sting punched straight through the metal just a few centimetres from his head.

'Make it quick!' Jay yelled as one end of the shutter buckled, popping out of its runner and numerous metallic tentacles began pushing through the gap. The writhing mass slowly forced the opening ever wider, just a metre away from where Rachel was still desperately fighting to brace the shutter.

'They're coming through!' Rachel yelled as Nat climbed up on the counter beside her and tried to help reinforce the barrier.

Sam ran to the rear of the storeroom and put his hand on the wall.

'Here goes nothing,' he said under his breath as he pulled one of the two remaining C4 charges from Jay's pack and placed it on the floor next to the wall. He tapped on the keypad attached to the charge, set the timer for thirty seconds and activated it. Sam slung Jay's pack over his shoulder and ran out of the storeroom, slamming the door behind him.

'Everybody, take cover,' he yelled as he ran back towards the others. 'Fire in the hole!'

'What?' Rachel gasped in astonishment. 'Are

you mad? Have you seen the size of this room? You're going to blow us all to pieces.'

'That's a chance we're going to have to take,' Sam said, pointing at the silver tentacles that were forcing their way around the buckling edges of the shutter. 'Anything's better than the alternative.'

'He has a point,' Jay said, leaping down from the counter and taking cover behind one of the stainless steel units. 'At least this way it'll be quick.'

Sam felt the blast a split second before he heard it as the concussion wave blew the heavy storeroom door clean off its hinges and sent it spinning across the room and slamming into the opposite wall. A sheet of flame roared out of the doorway and raced across the ceiling and Sam felt the heat on his face as he forced himself to his feet.

'Move!' he yelled at the others and began to pick his way through the burning debris towards the shattered remains of the storeroom doorway. He held his breath and stepped into the smoke-filled room, praying that the explosion had been powerful enough. The smoke began to clear and he felt a wave of relief when he saw a ragged hole in the back wall. He ran up to the hole and kicked at a couple of the loose cinder blocks around the edge, widening the gap just enough for someone to crawl through.

'Come on, through here,' Sam said as the others hurried into the room. Nat went first, crawling on her belly, quickly followed by Rachel. From the other room, there was a groaning crash as the steel shutter finally gave way under the combined assault of the Hunters and the shock wave from the explosion.

'You first,' Jay said, raising his rifle and pointing

101

it at the storeroom doorway, the buzzing of the Hunters grew louder.

'No,' Sam said, pulling the last C4 charge from the backpack. 'Go. I'll be right behind you.'

Jay hesitated, just for a moment, and then dived through the hole in the wall, dragging himself over the still-hot rubble. Sam watched Jay's boots disappear and set the timer on the charge for five seconds before tossing it back towards the door. He threw himself through the hole, scrambling out into the cool night air. He dragged himself out of the narrow opening and took cover a split second before there was a deep, muffled thump from the other side of the wall and a fireball roared out of the hole. He climbed to his feet and set off after the others who were already sprinting down the broad ramp that led away from the stadium. He knew that the final explosive charge would probably only have bought them a few seconds' head start. As if to confirm his fears, he heard a buzzing behind him as the first of the Hunters began to follow them outside. He didn't look back; knowing how close their pursuers were would make no difference. He just ran for his life.

As the sound of the Hunters grew louder and louder, Sam looked at his three friends running ahead of him and with a sudden, cold certainty he knew exactly what he had to do. He stopped running, turned and raised his rifle, aiming at the swarm of Hunters that were now only twenty metres away. He'd never be able to stop them, but he might slow them down. When the swarm raced towards him, he could have sworn he heard their angry screams *inside* his head. He squeezed the trigger, growling through gritted teeth as he

102

emptied the rifle's magazine into the silver-skinned creatures, sending spurts of viscous green blood spraying into the air. Despite the hail of bullets, the swarm hardly slowed as it bore down upon him. The other three members of the Ops Team slowed, turning and looking back to see what was happening.

'Sam!' Rachel screamed. 'No!'

At the base of the black spire in the centre of the stadium a digital counter hit zero.

Sam heard a distant explosion and felt a tremor run through the ground underfoot. The Hunters all screeched in unison and then fell out of the air, hitting the ground and sliding and tumbling towards him, their tentacles flailing uselessly. Moments later, the ground in front of Sam was covered with the fallen creatures. Sam lowered his rifle, staring in amazement at the dead swarm. The sound in his head was gone. The others ran back towards him, Rachel in the lead, with a furious expression on her face. She ran up to Sam and punched him hard on the shoulder.

'You bloody idiot,' she said angrily. 'What the hell do you think you were doing?'

'Ow,' Sam said, rubbing his shoulder. 'I was just trying to buy you some time.'

'That's not how this works,' Rachel snapped. 'We've already lost one person tonight. There aren't enough of us left for you to just go throwing your life away like that.'

'Hey, Rach, chill,' Jay said as he walked up beside them. 'He was trying to do the right thing.'

'Whatever,' Rachel said, turning and marching off with an exasperated sigh, heading back towards the tunnel access.

'Thanks,' Sam said to Jay as they watched Rachel walk away.

'Hey, don't thank me,' Jay said with a smile. 'I agree with her. You're an idiot. Brave, but definitely still an idiot.'

'What happened to them?' Nat asked, crouching down and poking one of the dead Hunters with the muzzle of her rifle.

'I have no idea,' Sam said, shaking his head. 'The charge in the stadium blew and then . . . well, see for yourself.'

'Are they dead?' Nat asked.

'I don't know. It certainly looks like it,' Sam replied with a shrug.

'Come on,' Jay said. 'We need to get out of here.' He pointed to the east where three points of green light could be clearly seen, growing steadily larger as they headed towards them.

'Looks like we've caught their attention at least,' Sam said.

'Not sure that's a good thing,' Nat said before standing up and jogging after Rachel.

'This might sound crazy,' Sam said, 'but I think we should take one of these things back for Stirling.'

'You're right,' Jay said with a nod. 'That *does* sound crazy.'

'Seriously,' Sam replied. 'I bet he's never got his hands on one that's dead but undamaged. It could be useful.'

Jay stared at him for a moment and then let out a long sigh.

'Just remember that this was your idea,' he said, shaking his head.

'Come on, give me a hand,' Sam said, taking

hold of one side of the upper carapace of the nearest fallen Hunter.

'Why do I get the feeling that I'm going to regret this?' Jay said, slinging his rifle over his shoulder and taking hold of the other side.

'Mind the stingers,' Sam said as he lifted the Hunter off the ground. It was surprisingly heavy for its size.

They walked quickly after the girls, carrying the Hunter between them. In the distance they could now hear the throbbing rumble of the approaching Threat drop-ships.

'What on earth are you doing with that thing?' Rachel asked as the boys entered the enclosed courtyard with their prize.

'Sam thought Stirling might cheer up a bit if we brought him a new pet,' Jay said. 'I suggested a puppy, but then we realised it might be difficult to take it for walks.'

'Very funny,' Rachel said, frowning. 'I suppose you geniuses have considered the possibility that it might not actually be dead?'

The boys looked at each other and then down at the Hunter.

'Ummm, no,' Jay said, suddenly sounding nervous. 'We hadn't actually thought about that to be honest.'

'Well, let's just make sure, shall we?' Rachel said, raising her rifle and pointing it at the Hunter.

'No, don't,' Sam said, holding up his free hand. 'The whole point of this is to bring one of these things back undamaged for Stirling.'

'He has a point, Rach,' Nat said. 'Stirling's never had a chance to look at a Hunter that's not been blown up or shot to pieces before.'

105

'OK,' Rachel said, lowering her rifle, 'but if that thing so much as twitches, I'm emptying a clip into it. Understood?'

'Understood,' Sam said with a nod.

'OK, now that's settled, can I suggest we get underground?' Jay said as the rumble of the Threat ships drew nearer. 'Because any minute now those things are going to start dropping Grendels, and I don't know about you guys, but I'd rather not still be here when that happens.'

'Fascinating,' Stirling said as he gently lifted the section he had cut out of the Hunter's shell and inspected what lay beneath, 'absolutely fascinating.'

'Glad you like it, Doc,' Jay said.

'Are you certain it's dead?' Jackson asked, eyeing the Hunter warily, his rifle lowered but ready.

'As certain as I can be with a creature with such an alien physiology,' Stirling replied. 'It really is quite unlike anything I've ever seen before. A seamless hybridisation of the organic and the mechanical. It's hard to say for sure if it was constructed or *grown*.'

'I don't care if it is dead,' Rachel said. 'Damn thing still give me the creeps.'

'You say the Hunters all deactivated simultaneously,' Stirling said, still staring at the creature.

'Yeah,' Sam replied, 'as soon as the transmitter inside the stadium blew, they all just hit the ground.'

106

'It sounds like some sort of catastrophic signal feedback loop,' Will said.

'Just what I was thinking,' Jay said, rolling his eyes.

'Either that or the transmitter was required to send instructions to the swarm,' Stirling said, frowning slightly. 'Which would suggest that there is a finite limit to how far they can travel from the Threat Mothership without the control signal being boosted in some way. I suspect that the signal would normally be relayed by Threat drop-ships in the area, but these new ground-based transmitters would provide a more permanent solution. It's hard to be certain since we have never managed to bring down one of the drop-ships and see what effect that might have on any Hunters in the area, but it would explain why we have not seen any of these transmitters before now.'

'Which means that we could take down every Hunter within range if we destroy the transmitters,' Rachel said.

'In theory, yes,' Stirling replied.

'Assuming we can find them,' Nat said.

'You were lucky not to take more casualties this time,' Jackson said. 'We had no idea we were sending you into a Hunter nest. Not to mention the fact that the Threat are bound to have increased security around any other transmitters they're putting up after what happened last night. That may have been our first and last chance to hit them like that.'

'I agree,' Stirling said. 'I cannot justify another operation like that, no matter how tempting the target may be. However, there is another option. Now that we know that the transmissions from

107

these towers are so vital to the control of the Hunters, we can try to find a way to block them.'

'Easier said than done,' Will said. 'It was the strength of those signals that led us to that transmitter in the first place. To jam even one of them would require ... well ... a lot more power than we have available.'

'Yes, William, you're quite right,' Stirling said with a nod, 'which is why we won't try to block the transmission of the signal; we block its *reception*.'

'Limit the range and lower the power consumption,' Anne said, nodding enthusiastically. 'If the electromagnetic interference ratio is reduced ...'

'And this is where they start talking science at each other,' Jay said with a sigh. 'I don't know about you guys, but I'm hungry.'

'Yeah,' Nat said, 'let's go and see what delights Toby's prepared for breakfast today.'

'If it's tinned grapefruit again, things could get violent,' Jay said with a grin as the pair of them walked out of the lab.

Sam and Rachel watched in silence as Stirling, Will and Anne continued their examination of the dead Hunter.

'Listen,' Rachel said quietly after a minute or two, 'I'm sorry about losing my temper with you back there. I appreciate what you were trying to do. It was just ... you know ... with losing Tim like that. I just ...' She trailed off.

'Hey, don't worry about it,' Sam said. 'You were right. It was a stupid thing to do. I'm just so sick of running from the Threat, I wanted to stand and fight for once. Jackson's right, though—we can't fight them like that. If that charge hadn't detonated when it did, I'd have ended up just like Tim. It's like Jackson always says, frightened but alive beats brave and dead every time.'

'True,' Rachel said, 'but I know what you mean about wanting to fight back. We can't go on living in holes underground for ever.'

'Maybe these guys will come up with something we can use to level the playing field slightly,' he said, gesturing towards Stirling, Will and Anne, who were deep in conversation. Jackson stood to one side, never taking his eyes off the Hunter on the bench.

'Well,' Sam said, 'I don't think I'm going to be much use here, so I'm going to hit the mess hall for breakfast before Jay cleans the place out.'

'Yeah, I'll come with you,' Rachel said, 'but, I tell you, if Jay starts going on about bacon again, I'm going to shoot him.'

Sam thought back to the incident when Jay had spent five minutes talking with such passion about the smell and taste of bacon that it actually still made his mouth water just thinking about it.

'Oh, if he does that again,' Sam said with a grin, 'you can use my gun.'

'Well, you guys certainly stirred up a hornet's nest,' Adam said as he walked towards the other Ops Team members. Behind him Kate walked through and then resealed the heavy steel door that led out into the tunnel system. They had left on a scouting mission several hours ago and had only just returned.

'What do you mean?' Rachel asked as Adam unslung his rifle and handed it to Jack.

'Well, Jackson asked us to go and take a look at what was happening around Wembley after last night and the place is absolutely crawling with Threat units now.'

'There's no chance we're getting anywhere near that place again. We counted four Grendels patrolling the perimeter and Hunter activity is off the scale.'

'But we destroyed the transmitter,' Jay said, frowning. 'How come there are still Hunters operating in the area?'

'I have no idea,' Kate said as she too passed her weapon to Jack, 'but the whole area's flooded with them now. We barely made it out undetected.'

'Maybe they've already got another transmitter up,' Rachel suggested.

'I was kinda hoping it would take them a little bit longer than that to recover,' Jay said with a sigh. 'Just giving them a blind spot for a few hours is hardly worth the price we paid.'

'You did more than that,' Jackson said as he approached. 'You demonstrated that we can hit them where they're vulnerable. The scale of their response shows that. That's why I sent Kate and Adam up there, so that I could get a better idea of just how badly we hurt them.'

'Oh, I think it's safe to say that we've got them pretty annoyed,' Kate said. 'That whole sector's going to be a no-go area for a while.'

'They've diverted their forces to defend one area, which means in turn that they're going to be more vulnerable everywhere else,' Jackson said with a grim smile. 'Now all we have to do is work

110

out where to hit them next and that's exactly what Doctor Stirling is doing right now.'

'Sounds good,' Jay said, 'assuming he doesn't send us into another Hunter nest.'

'You're right, Jay, about the price being too high,' Jackson said with a nod. 'We all know that we can't afford *any* losses. We are too few and they are too many.'

'So where and when do we attack them next?' Rachel asked.

'When?' Jackson said. 'Soon. Where?' He moved over to the map of London that was hanging on the wall and pointed at the huge circle in the centre of the city which represented the position of the Threat Mothership. 'Right where it will hurt them the most.'

7

'Here's what we know,' Stirling said, addressing the members of the Ops Team gathered in the briefing room. 'The Mothership is the hub of Threat activity in the area. All of the Threat aircraft are based there and the material that is gathered by the enslaved humans is delivered directly to it. There is evidence to suggest that there are similar vessels located throughout the rest of the country and, indeed, throughout the world. My research into the transmissions from the vessel over London has led me to conclude that collectively these ships are all just nodes in one giant planetary network. That network was used to transmit what I call the Primary Signal, and it was this signal that allowed the Threat to take instant mental control of the vast majority of the Earth's population. Thanks to the efforts of the Operations team in retrieving an intact sample of one of the Threat Hunters and destroying one of their command transmitters, we have begun to make significant progress in understanding exactly how the Threat forces are controlled. More significantly, we have also begun to understand how it might be possible to interrupt that control.'

'Doc, this is all really interesting,' Jay said, 'but it's not making the idea of half a dozen of us attacking a three-kilometre-wide Threat Mothership that just happens to be the heart of the entire Threat army in London sound any less insane.'

'Thank you, Jacob,' Stirling said, raising an eyebrow. 'I was coming to that. An all-out assault would obviously be a suicidal act of madness. What I am proposing instead is an infiltration mission to access the mechanism at the heart of the Threat command and control network. If we succeed in gaining access to that system, we can then turn the Threat's own weapons against them. That's the only way we can realistically hope to defeat them.'

'Are you seriously suggesting that not only do we have to actually get on board the Mothership, but once we do we just wander into their central command and control centre and blow the place up?' Rachel asked. 'I don't mean to sound negative, but I'm still finding it hard to see how this plan doesn't fall into the "suicidal act of madness" category.'

'Oh, we won't be blowing anything up, even though I know how much you enjoy it,' Stirling said with a smile. 'No, we're going to be doing something more subtle than that. I've nearly perfected a new weapon, something that will finally allow us to fight the Threat effectively. If we can deliver that weapon to just the right place, we might finally be able to take back the city.'

'So what is this weapon?' Sam asked.

'All in good time, Samuel,' Stirling replied. 'The first priority is to establish precisely how we're going to infiltrate the Mothership. To do that we need to carry out a detailed reconnaissance of the area directly below the vessel where the enslaved humans bring the materials they gather for their masters.'

'That's not going to be easy,' Adam said. 'We've never got that close to the heart of Threat territory before. We'll be walking straight into the lion's den.'

'I understand that it will be difficult and dangerous,' Stirling replied, 'but if we are going to find a way on to the Threat command vessel, that is the most likely route. The Threat must have a way of transporting the gathered materials to the Mothership and, whatever that mechanism is, it might just provide a way for us to get on board the vessel without being detected.'

'OK, so who gets to go and spy on the neighbours?' Jay asked.

'Normally I'd use Adam and Kate for a reconnaissance mission like this,' Jackson replied, 'but there's a good chance this could very quickly turn from a quiet look-see to a full-on combat operation, so I'm going to send you and Sam.'

'What about us?' Rachel asked, sharing the same look of irritation as Nat.

'You and Nat are staying here,' Jackson said. 'I don't want to send you all on a mission like this. The key will be keeping a low profile and four people are twice as likely to attract unwanted attention as two. Besides, if this all goes wrong, and it might, I don't want to lose the entire Ops Team in one fell swoop.'

'Thanks,' Jay said with a crooked smile. 'It's always nice to know that you're expendable.'

'I'm not suggesting you are,' Jackson said, shaking his head, 'but at the same time we do have to be realistic about the inherent risks in a mission like this.'

'When do we leave?' Sam asked, trying to hide the sudden twinge of nervousness he felt.

'Tonight,' Jackson said. 'I know it's short notice, but it's best that we do this while the Threat are still distracted by last night's events. With a bit of luck we'll catch them looking in the wrong direction.'

'Or they'll have doubled their security measures,' Rachel said, 'and, if that's the case, the more guns we have on our side the better.'

'I understand your frustration, Rachel,' Jackson said, 'but I've made my decision and this is not and has never been a democracy. Do I make myself clear?'

'As crystal, *sir*,' Rachel replied with a frown, her tone icy.

'Good,' Jackson replied. 'Sam, Jay, Doctor Stirling would like you to remain here—the rest of you are dismissed.'

The others filed out as Stirling beckoned the two boys over to the other side of the room.

'I think that this might be a good opportunity

for you to field test a new piece of equipment that we've put together,' Stirling said, gesturing to a small metallic cylinder on the table behind him.

'This is our new super-weapon?' Jay asked, looking doubtful.

'Oh no, this is something else,' Stirling explained. 'We got the idea when the Hunters attacked you last night.'

'What is it?' Sam asked, looking at the device curiously.

'This is a short-range signal jammer that's designed to block the electromagnetic signal used to control the Hunters,' Stirling said, picking up the device. 'You flip the lid open like this, and press the button underneath. Its range is only about ten metres and it only has enough charge for one use, but it should instantly disable any Hunters within range when activated.'

'Should?' Jay said with a frown.

'Well, it is experimental,' Stirling replied, 'but the theory behind it is sound.'

'I dunno, Doc,' Jay said. 'I've always found that my rifle's pretty good at disabling Hunters. I think I might just stick with that if you don't mind.'

'Yes, I appreciate your fondness for firearms,' Stirling said, 'but they don't work silently and they don't disable however many Hunters happen to be in range all at the same time.'

'He has a point, Jay,' Sam said, taking the jammer from Stirling. 'This would have come in very handy the other night.' The image of the swarm of Hunters flying straight at him outside Wembley was still fresh in his mind.

'All right,' Jay said. 'Can't hurt to take it with us, I suppose.'

'Remember, just one shot,' Stirling said. 'After that it's useless.'

'Got it,' Sam said. 'Thanks.'

'Come on,' Jay said. 'I want to go and pick Adam and Kate's brains about the best route to get us up close to that thing without getting spotted.'

Sam slipped the jammer into the thigh pocket of his combat trousers and the two boys headed for the door.

'Good luck, gentlemen,' Stirling said as they left. 'Stay safe.'

'Rachel really wasn't very happy, was she?' Sam said, his torch illuminating the pitch-black tunnel ahead of them.

'That's one way of putting it,' Jay said with a grin. 'Man, if looks could kill, Jackson would just be a smouldering spot on the floor right now.'

'Can't say I'd object to having the girls here too, though,' Sam said. 'Got a feeling that this might be the sort of job where two more pairs of eyes might come in really handy.'

'Not to mention two more rifles,' Jay replied.

'I dunno,' Sam said, 'that close to the Mothership, if we end up in a shooting match, I think we're going to find ourselves outgunned very quickly.'

'Yeah, right, let's just try and keep things nice and quiet.'

'So where does this tunnel bring us out?'

'Right underneath the Houses of Parliament,' Jay said. 'Hey, I've just realised, we're gonna be just like Guy Fawkes, just with C4 instead of gunpowder.'

'Probably best if we don't actually blow anything up, though,' Sam said with a chuckle. 'Seeing as how we're trying to avoid detection and all that.'

'You're starting to sound almost as boring as Jackson,' Jay replied. 'You didn't seem to mind a little bit of explosive destruction at Wembley the other night.'

'True, but it was either that or being ripped to pieces by a swarm of Hunters, so I think it was probably OK under the circumstances.'

'If you say so. Personally I reckon you like blowing stuff up just as much as I do.'

'Shhh,' Sam said suddenly, holding a finger to his lips. 'Do you hear that?'

From somewhere in the darkness ahead of them they could hear a low throbbing rumble.

'Yeah, I hear it. What is it?' Jay asked.

'No idea,' Sam said, crouching down and placing his palm flat on the dusty tunnel floor. The ground was trembling very slightly, the vibrations increasing and diminishing in time with the sound. They continued walking for another few minutes and began to feel the vibrations through the soles of their boots.

'How far to the exit point?' Sam asked.

'I'm not sure. Can't be more than half a kilometre or so. It was only eight hundred metres from that last junction,' Jay replied.

'OK, let's keep moving,' Sam said, starting to feel nervous again. 'We want to keep it quiet from here on in. Kill the torches and switch to your NV goggles.'

Sam switched off his light, turned on his

night-vision goggles and the tunnel ahead of them was illuminated in a gentle green glow. They moved quickly and quietly until they reached an iron gate that was secured with a heavy padlock.

'It's all right,' Jay said. 'I've got a key.' He took his backpack off and rummaged around inside before pulling out a pair of heavy bolt cutters. A couple of seconds later the padlock clattered to the ground and Jay pulled the gate open, its hinges squeaking in protest. They passed through the gate and found themselves in a circular chamber with other tunnels leading off from it in all directions.

'Where now?' Sam asked.

'Your guess is as good as mine,' Jay said, looking around the room. 'The maps we've got cover most of the tunnel system under the city, but there are no maps for some places, especially high-security locations like this.'

Sam looked around the chamber and spotted the security cameras and motion sensors mounted on the walls. They reminded him that the Parliament building above them would have once had some of the heaviest security in the country. Long dead and useless now, of course.

'Well, I guess we just follow our noses, then,' Sam said, and set off down the tunnel straight in front of him. They passed numerous doors set in the walls, all labelled with the titles of various high-ranking government officials. Doubtless these offices would have once served as a secure location for ministers and their aides during times of crisis or threat. Nobody had considered the possibility that the whole mechanism of government would be rendered irrelevant in the blink of an eye, that all these 'powerful' men and women could be reduced

118

to mindless slaves in the space of a heartbeat, no different to anyone else. They rounded a corner and Sam was relieved to see that at the far end there was a metal spiral staircase leading upwards.

'Up we go,' Sam whispered. 'Keep your eyes open. Remember, we have no idea what's waiting for us up there.'

They crept up the stairs, which led up to a solid-looking wooden door that was closed but thankfully unlocked. Sam opened the door a crack and looked through. There was no sign of anyone or, more importantly, any*thing* on the other side of the door and he pushed it open and headed through. They found themselves in a grand corridor with a tiled floor and ornately carved stonework on the ceiling and walls. Perhaps more than any other place that he had been since the arrival of the Threat, these echoing empty corridors in all their grandeur gave him the sense of how completely the alien invaders had stripped humanity of its power to determine its own future.

'Came here on a tour with my school once,' Jay said. 'Never imagined I'd be wandering around the place with a gun one day.'

'Well, unfortunately, this isn't really the time for sightseeing,' Sam said. 'If we're going to get a really good look at what the Threat are doing around here, then we need to get up high.' He glanced at a sign on the wall that had arrows pointing to various locations within the building. 'Come on, follow me.'

They ran through the empty corridors, the sound of their boots on the tiled floor echoing off the walls. The rumbling noise coming from outside was now even louder.

'There,' Sam said, pointing at an unassuming

119

wood and glass door set in the wall. Next to it was a sign that read 'Clock Tower'.

'You know, I can still remember the first time that I realised that this thing had stopped chiming,' Jay said as they hurried up the stairs inside the tower. 'I couldn't tell you exactly when it stopped, just when I noticed it had. Made me kinda sad to be honest.'

They continued up the tower until they reached a door marked 'Mechanism Room'. Walking inside, they saw the mass of black cogs, flywheels and springs that formed the mechanism for the giant clock at the ticking heart of Big Ben. It sat motionless now beneath the crossed spindles that passed through the walls of the room and out to each of the four clock faces. There were no windows in the room that would give them a view of what was going on outside.

'Looks like we need to keep going up,' Sam said. They climbed another flight of stairs, towards the belfry, feeling the cold night air on their faces as they stepped outside. The giant bells that had once chimed the famous tune that was so familiar to all Londoners hung inside a wire cage and Sam could only imagine how loud they would sound if you were this close to them when they rang. Assuming that actually ever happens again, he reminded himself. They passed by the bells and reached a final spiral staircase leading to the highest point of the tower, where a view of the dark city stretched out beneath them in all directions. Sam walked over to the wire mesh that surrounded the lantern and peered down at the scene directly below.

'Oh my God,' Jay said as he came and stood next to Sam and saw what was left of a broad swathe

120

of central London. Where St James's Park had once been there was now a charred crater. Within that crater tens of thousands, maybe hundreds of thousands of people were working under bright floodlights to build *something*. It looked a lot like an impossibly large version of the transmission spire that they'd discovered at Wembley. It was the source of the deafening rumbling sound that filled the air, its central sections lit by a pulsing green light that matched the rhythm of the sound precisely. Sam pulled off his night-vision googles and retrieved the binoculars from his backpack. The construction was made up of hundreds of giant matt black slabs, with large sections missing from the outer skin allowing Sam to see the people who were working within the brightly lit interior of the structure.

He turned his attention to the crater and saw that the steep rock walls at its edges were also covered with people who were hacking away at the rock with hand tools, slowly, but relentlessly making it ever larger. Beyond the crater huge teams of Walkers were working to systematically demolish even the largest buildings, clearing a path for the expansion of the crater. Sam tried very hard not to think about the fact that any one of the countless slaves labouring to complete whatever the Threat were building might have been his sister, or one of his parents. He had never given up hope of finding them. He turned his attention back to the centre of the structure where a single black spire, taller than any of the surrounding structures, reached up towards the sky. No, not the sky, Sam thought, as he looked up for the first time. Where the sky should have been was the underside of the Threat Mothership, its surface illuminated by waves of pulsing green light. He could see dozens of the black triangular drop-ships buzzing around the giant vessel, looking like gnats in comparison to the vast scale of the Mothership. He had never stood directly beneath it before and he suddenly realised that up close like this it made him feel very small and insignificant.

'There must be hundreds of Hunters mixed in amongst the humans,' Jay said, taking the binoculars and scanning the city below. 'Not to mention what looks like twenty or thirty Grendels patrolling the outer perimeter.'

'So how do we get inside?' Sam asked. 'We need to find out what that thing is.'

'Well, we're not fighting our way in, that's for sure,' Jay said, shaking his head. 'Besides which, how exactly do you plan to work out what that thing is? It's not like we're just going to be able to walk up and ask one of the Grendels to give us a guided tour, and somehow I doubt that they're going to have left a set of blueprints, helpfully labelled in English, lying around anywhere.'

'I don't know,' Sam said. 'I was just thinking that if we could get a closer look and some pictures maybe it'll give Stirling something to go on.'

'All right,' Jay said, holding his hands up, 'but if this goes pear-shaped I'm throwing you at the nearest Grendel and running, OK?'

'Sounds reasonable,' Sam said with a smile.

Jackson walked into Dr Stirling's lab and closed the

door behind him. He crossed over to the bench and watched as Stirling carefully placed a tiny circuit board into the top of the foot long silver cylinder. He closed the hatch and it sealed with a tiny hiss of escaping air.

'Is it ready?' Jackson asked.

'Yes,' Stirling replied, removing his glasses and rubbing at his tired eyes. 'The more important question, though, is will it work?'

'Let's hope so, for all our sakes,' Jackson said, 'because we don't have many more cards to play. Unless, of course, you've found a new group of kids that you're not telling me about.'

'No, no new subjects, I'm afraid,' Stirling replied. 'None of the towers have picked up a new implant signal for months. Apart from Mr Riley, of course. I fear we must assume that the others were lost to the Threat. If only we'd had more warning. We were supposed to have had time to prepare.'

'We've had this conversation a hundred times, Iain,' Jackson said, shaking his head. 'This was nobody's fault.'

'We both know that's not entirely true,' Stirling said. 'Indeed, if things had worked out slightly differently, I might have been part of the problem. Instead of which I'm now the one who's trying desperately to find a solution.'

'That was a long time ago. If you'd known then what we know now about the Foundation, there's no way you would have been involved. Iain, once we knew the truth, we did the right thing. You, me, we did everything we could to stop them with the resources we had. It just all happened too soon. Who knows, maybe this thing,' he nodded towards the silver cylinder, 'can make it right again.'

'I just wish Daniel could have been here to see how important his work has been in making this possible, Robert,' Stirling said. 'Whether he intended it or not, in that boy he's given us our best hope. It may not be enough to take back the planet, but at least it's enough to give us hope that one day that might at least be possible.'

'And at this point,' Jackson said, 'that's really all we can ask for.'

8

'Are you serious?' Jay said, looking at Sam with an expression of disbelief, pacing back and forth across the office on the edge of St James's Park that they had broken into a few minutes earlier.

'It's the only way,' Sam said, handing Jay his rifle and taking off his backpack. He slid the compact digital camera that Stirling had given them into the pocket of his trousers and removed his shoulder holster, placing it on the desk next to him.

'Look, I hear what you're saying,' Jay said, 'but this is insane. You're going to get yourself killed.'

'You saw how many people there are down there,' Sam said, pointing through the window at the glow from the nearby Threat construction site. 'Do you really think they're going to notice one more mindless zombie wandering around the place?'

'Yeah, actually, I do,' Jay replied, 'and when they find you they're either going to throw you to the Grendels or brain-wipe you.'

'I think we've probably established by now that

124

we're immune to the Threat control signal,' Sam said.

'Great, so it'll be the Grendel stomping, then,' Jay said, sounding irritated. 'At least let me go and find a bucket so that I'll be able to take you home with me.'

Sam heard a noise in his head, a low guttural growling sound.

'Do you hear that?' he asked.

'Hear what?'

'Like a growling sound.'

'All I can hear is the racket that the Threat building is making,' Jay said. 'No growl . . .'

They both ducked as they felt a rhythmic thud through the floor and a few seconds later a Grendel walked down the street outside, just a few metres from where they were hiding. The growling got louder as it passed and then diminished as it walked away. Sam realised that whatever the sound that the Threat creatures made inside his head was, he was the only one who could hear it. It had started happening after he had recovered from the Hunter sting and he decided that when they got back he would have to discuss it with Stirling.

'This is such a bad idea,' Jay whispered. 'Really, really deep down, one-of-a-kind, has-no-equal, dumb.'

'Now you're just being negative,' Sam said with a grin as he stood up and unbolted the sash window.

'OK, if you're insisting on going in there, then I'm coming with you,' Jay said, placing his rifle on the desk.

'No, you're not,' Sam said, shaking his head. 'If I don't make it out of there, you're the only person who can report back and tell Stirling what the

Threat are up to here. If we both get caught, then all this will have been for nothing. Besides two of us are much more likely to get spotted than one.'

Jay stared at him for a moment or two before letting out a long sigh.

'OK, you're right, but I still think it's a bad idea, especially without back-up. At least take this with you,' Jay said, taking Sam's pistol from the holster on the desk and handing it to him.

'OK, if it'll stop you worrying like a little old lady,' Sam said with a smile, taking the gun and tucking it into the waistband of his trousers in the small of his back, where it was hidden by his T-shirt.

Sam turned back to the window, slid the heavy wooden frame upwards and climbed through. He landed silently on the pavement outside and watched the back of the patrolling Grendel for a few seconds as it continued up the street. As soon as the giant creature was far enough away, Sam sprinted across the road and climbed quickly over the railings surrounding the park. He landed in the bushes on the other side and waited for a moment before creeping forward through the foliage until he could peek through the leaves at what lay beyond. There were twenty metres of open ground covered in overgrown grass between him and the crater but there were also, thankfully, no Hunters hovering nearby. He took a deep breath and ran towards the edge of the crater. When he was just a few metres from the drop, he threw himself forward, landing flat on his belly in the long grass. He crawled carefully up to the edge and peeked over. Below him a group of Walkers was working at the rock face, pickaxes and sledgehammers

126

slowly breaking up the stone and soil, while other blank-faced people shovelled the rubble into wheelbarrows and tubs, which they slowly pushed or dragged away towards the centre of the crater.

Sam heard a faint buzzing inside his head and looked around quickly. Off to his left, he saw a group of Walkers escorted by a single Hunter walking in his direction along the edge of the crater. There was no time for hesitation. He dropped over the edge of the crater, sliding on his back down the loose soil and gravel and landing in the middle of the group working to expand the crater. Just as he had hoped, none of the people paid him the slightest attention; instead they just remained totally focused on their tasks.

Sam got slowly to his feet and looked around, doing his best to mimic the blank, emotionally neutral expression that all the Walkers shared. He saw a large plastic tub nearby and slowly walked over to it. He saw a woman carrying a similar container approach a man who was shovelling up the rubble produced by the people working on the crater wall. Sam followed her, waiting patiently as the man shovelled dirt into her tub before stepping forward and having his container filled as well. Once the tub was full Sam set off after the woman, following her but maintaining a steady pace, his eyes staring ahead, desperately resisting the urge to look around. He knew if there was one thing that might alert a Hunter to his real state of mind it would be any indication of simple human curiosity.

He followed the woman deeper and deeper into the construction site as she headed towards a huge opening, ten metres tall, in the wall of one of the outermost black structures. They walked inside and entered a cavernous space lined on all sides with machines that looked like enormous high-tech furnaces—black cylinders three metres across with a large square opening in the front that glowed with a pale purple light. Hovering in the air in the centre of the area was a single Hunter, its multifaceted eyes twitching and rotating as it surveyed the activity below. Beneath the creature, dozens of Walkers queued at each furnace, taking turns dumping the soil and gravel that they carried into the glowing portals before walking back the way they'd come, presumably to retrieve another load. Sam followed suit, waiting his turn and dutifully tipping the box full of rubble he was carrying into the machine. The light within flared more brightly for a second and there was a short sharp hiss as the rocks and soil vaporised, filling the air around him with a faint, acrid odour. He turned and walked under the floating Hunter, silently praying that he had not done anything that might attract its attention. He headed back the way he'd just come and caught sight of the woman he'd been following before, on her way back to make another collection. He trailed her for a minute or so, but as he passed a dark, partially constructed section of the Threat structure he turned ninety degrees to his left and walked straight into the waiting shadows. Once he was out of sight he put the waste container on the ground and waited, ears straining for any sound of pursuing Hunters. After thirty seconds or so he let out a relieved sigh.

'OK,' Sam muttered to himself, 'now let's see if we can work out just what these alien creeps are up to.'

He crept further inside, walking down a

darkened, half-finished corridor towards a dim light that was coming from round a corner. He could hear a faint tapping noise as he approached and he turned the corner to find a brainwashed man working alone, bolting a panel to the wall. Sam walked past him, heading still deeper into the structure. He walked for fifteen minutes, following the same corridor, feeling that he was now on a very gradual downward slope and the air in the corridor seemed to be getting warmer and drier.

Suddenly, he felt a buzzing in his skull and a few seconds later he heard the sound of approaching Hunters. He quickly ran back up the corridor and ducked into a gloomy side passage, crouching in the shadows behind a column of pipes as the sounds of the Hunters got nearer and nearer. From his hiding place he saw several Hunters race down the main corridor and back out the way he had just come. As the sound of the Hunters faded into the distance, Sam came out from behind the pipes. Just as he was about to walk back out into the corridor a bulkhead hissed down from the ceiling and slammed shut with a clang, blocking his path. Sam turned back towards the darkened passage behind him as the lights in the ceiling lit up one by one, creating a path for him.

'Well, this can't be good,' Sam said to himself. The lights along the corridor continued to switch on just ahead of him. He hoped that it might be some sort of automated system, but he had a horrible feeling that it wasn't. He suddenly felt very much like a lab rat trapped in a maze. He walked down the corridor for a couple more minutes. The air around was still growing steadily warmer and the persistent throbbing rumble that he had heard all night was louder. The end of the corridor came into view, sealed by a heavy metal door. The bulkhead hissed open as he approached and he was hit by a wave of stifling heat and deafening noise. He walked through the door and found himself standing on a gantry running along the wall of an enormous room. Above him, mounted on the ceiling, was an enormous spherical machine, at least a hundred metres in diameter, its surface pulsing with the same green light that he had seen lighting up the exterior of the structure. Hanging from the bottom of the machine was a semi-transparent crystalline barrel that seemed to be focusing the sizzling, green beam that speared out of the machine and down into the pit below. Sam stepped up to the railing at the edge of the gantry and felt a moment of dizzying vertigo as he stared down into the vast chasm, its bottom filled with bubbling magma, hundreds of metres below him. The heat that filled the air was rising up from the vast geological wound that this machine had torn in the surface of the Earth. Sam could not help but feel a sense of awe as he tried to take in the monumental scale of the machine and the immense power that it was channelling. A movement further along the gantry suddenly caught Sam's attention.

Standing there was a man in a white linen suit with long curly dark hair that was streaked with grey. He was staring straight at Sam and there was a cryptic smile on his face. He pulled what looked like a mobile phone out of the inside pocket of his suit and spoke into it for a few seconds, even though Sam knew that was impossible. The entire cellular network had stopped working just days after the Threat had arrived. The man finished his brief conversation and placed the phone back in his pocket. Sam turned back towards the open door behind him, but a split second later it slid shut with a solid thunk. Reluctantly, he turned back towards the mysterious stranger and the man beckoned for Sam to follow him before walking along the gantry towards a door at the far end. Sam followed the man into a tastefully decorated office, completely at odds with the alien architecture. The man sat down behind the antique desk that stood in the middle of the room and gestured for Sam to take the seat opposite.

'Who are you?' Sam asked, fighting to remain calm despite the feeling of panic in his gut.

'I think I'll ask the questions, my young friend,' the man replied with a smile. 'Please, sit.'

'No, thanks,' Sam said, pulling the concealed pistol from the small of his back and levelling it at the stranger. 'Now, why don't you answer my question. Who are you?'

'Oh, how very disappointing. I was hoping for slightly more than an adolescent thug waving a gun around,' the man said, still smiling. 'My name is Oliver Fletcher, and I assume you're part of the resistance group that has been such a thorn in our side recently.'

'What's that thing out there?' Sam asked, ignoring Fletcher's question. 'What are the Threat building here?'

'The Threat?' Fletcher laughed. 'Is that what your pathetic little band of freedom fighters is calling them? Their true name is unpronounceable in our language, but the name they have given themselves in English is the Voidborn and this planet is and always has been theirs.'

131

'What are you talking about?' Sam demanded, keeping his gun trained on Fletcher.

'We're just caretakers,' Fletcher said, his smile suddenly fading, 'an engineered workforce that will help with the harvest when the time comes. That's all we've ever been.'

'And I'm supposed to believe that, am I?' Sam snapped at Fletcher. 'Coming from someone who's actually working *with* these things.'

'You can believe whatever you wish,' Fletcher said with a shrug. 'It makes no difference to me or indeed to the ultimate fate of the Earth. Now, I'd really appreciate it if you told me absolutely everything you know about your comrades-in-arms. Shall we start with the location of whatever rock they're hiding under?'

'In case you hadn't noticed, I'm the one with the gun,' Sam said.

'A gun which you're going to give to me,' Fletcher said, reaching forward and touching a crystalline disc in the centre of the desk. 'Or I shall have my sentries rip your friend to pieces right in front of your eyes.' The air above the crystal disc shimmered for a second and then solidified into a three-dimensional projection of Jay standing between two Hunters, their tentacles wrapped round his arms. 'Did you really think that you would be able to get within a hundred metres of this facility without being detected? I've been watching your every move for the past half an hour.'

'Call off your Hunters and let Jay go or I put a bullet in your skull,' Sam said, cocking the hammer on his pistol.

'Hunters? Yes, I suppose that's what they

132

must seem like to you,' Fletcher said. 'No, I won't tell the Hunters to release your friend. What's actually going to happen, is that you're going to put your gun down, so that we can continue your interrogation in a more civilised manner.' Sam felt a sudden buzzing in his head and the door behind him hissed open. Three Hunters floated into the room, the barrels of the energy weapons mounted in their upper carapaces glowing with green light. 'You *can* still shoot me, of course. You may very well kill me,' Fletcher said, 'but then these Hunters will vaporise you where you stand and your friend will die in agony.' His voice turned suddenly cold, a look of pure malevolence filling his eyes. 'Now put the gun *down!*' The last word was a barked command, not a request.

Sam hesitated for a moment. It would be so easy to squeeze the trigger, but what would that achieve? Jackson's words echoed through his mind.

Frightened but alive beats brave and dead every time.

Sam uncocked the pistol and laid it on the desk in front of him.

'You see,' Fletcher said, the smile returning to his face, 'that wasn't so hard, was it?'

Fletcher stood up and walked round the desk. He closed his eyes for a second and the buzzing that Sam could feel in his head was joined by a whispering voice, speaking in an unintelligible language. Immediately, the two Hunters wrapped their tentacles round Sam's upper arms, their grip painfully tight.

Fletcher walked towards the door, which hissed open as he approached, with the Hunters dragging Sam along behind him.

133

'This is only the beginning,' Fletcher said as they walked up a broad corridor lined with black techno-organic panels, illuminated with patterns of flickering green light. 'Soon facilities just like this one will have been built in every corner of the world. Everything will be ready for their arrival.'

'Whose arrival?' Sam asked.

'Oh, I wouldn't want to spoil the surprise,' Fletcher said. 'Don't worry, you and your friends won't be around to see it anyway, so it really doesn't concern you.'

'Why would you do this?' Sam said. 'Why would you cooperate with these, what did you call them, Voidborn?'

'The oldest reason in the book,' Fletcher replied. 'Survival.'

They walked towards a huge pair of double doors made from the same matt black material that covered the outside of the Voidborn structure. These slowly rumbled apart and the corridor was filled with the sounds of the enslaved humans labouring within the compound. Fletcher walked ahead of them, heading for the large building where earlier Sam had seen the slaves dumping the rubble from their excavations. In the centre of the brightly lit area, Jay stood between a pair of Hunters, just as he had appeared in the projection on Fletcher's desk.

'Sam!' Jay yelled as he saw his friend approaching. His expression changed to a confused frown as he turned his attention to Fletcher. 'And who the hell are you?'

'You may call me Mr Fletcher,' he replied. 'Now, shall we get down to business?' He walked over to a slave who was queueing up to dump his load of rubble into one of the black furnaces that lined the room and took a fist-sized rock from the container he was carrying. He walked towards the glowing portal at the front of the furnace and tossed the rock inside and it vanished with a flash.

'Really quite a remarkable piece of Voidborn technology,' Fletcher said, 'capable of full molecular disintegration. Everything that enters the energy field is broken down at the molecular level and then harvested to be used as raw materials in the nano-forges. Absolutely nothing is wasted—true lossless recycling. I'm sure you can imagine the effect that it would have on human tissue.' He turned back towards Sam and Jay.

'Is he working *with* these things?' Jay asked Sam, shaking his head in disbelief.

'I'm afraid so,' Sam said, staring at Fletcher.

'Do you want to know what I really hate, Sam?' Fletcher asked. 'I really hate being threatened, especially by a boy. So here's how this is going to work. Your friend Jay is going to tell me exactly where the rest of your little friends are holed up right now, or I'm going to feed you piece by piece into that disintegration field while he watches.'

'Don't tell him anything, Jay,' Sam said as the Hunters dragged him towards the portal.

'Where are your friends?' Fletcher asked Jay. Jay spat on the floor at Fletcher's feet and said nothing. 'Have it your way.' He turned back to the Hunters restraining Sam and closed his eyes for a second. Again Sam heard the whispering inside his skull and a moment later the Hunters began to drag him closer to the furnace, raising his right arm and pushing his hand towards the crackling energy field.

'Last chance,' Fletcher said. 'Tell me where the rest of the resistance is based or your friend loses his arm. And that will just be the beginning.'

'You don't have to do this,' Jay said. 'Please, I . . .'

'Are you going to tell me or not!' Fletcher yelled.

'No,' Jay said, hanging his head. 'I'm not.'

'Very well,' Fletcher said, turning back towards the Hunters and closing his eyes again.

Sam fought with every ounce of his strength against the Hunter holding his arm as it pushed his right hand towards the disintegration field, but it was no good; the creature was simply too strong. He felt the hairs on the back of his arm stand up as his fingers moved to within millimetres of the field.

Suddenly, there was the sound of an explosion in the distance, followed almost instantly by the sound of automatic gunfire. The Hunter that had been pushing Sam's arm into the furnace was torn apart by a hail of bullets, sending hot green liquid spraying across Sam's face and chest. The Hunter's tentacles went slack and Sam wrenched his arm free of its grip as the creature holding his other arm shrieked in enraged alarm. Moments later there was the sound of another explosion from somewhere much closer, and the night sky in the compound outside was lit up by a billowing fireball. The Hunter holding Sam's other arm released its grip and spun backwards through the air, twitching and jerking as it too was hit by another burst of fire. Sam pulled himself free and spun round just in time to see Rachel and Nat advancing into the room, rifles raised. A moment later they fired in unison at the Hunters hovering above Jay, taking them both down.

'Catch!' Rachel yelled, and pulled the pistol from the holster on her belt, throwing it to Sam. He caught the weapon and raised it, aiming at one of the other Hunters that had been supervising the slaves as they emptied their loads of rubble into the furnaces. He pulled the trigger and the pistol bucked twice in his hands in quick succession, hitting the Hunter dead centre and sending it spinning straight into one of the nearby disintegration fields, where it vanished with a flash. Jay untangled himself from the twitching tentacles of the two dead Hunters that were wrapped round his arms and ran towards Nat who tossed her own side-arm to him. Fletcher made a break for it, running for cover as two more Hunters that had been on guard started to return fire at the four armed humans. Sizzling green energy bolts flashed through the air, sending the two girls diving for cover behind the furnaces. Sam kept firing, moving towards Rachel's position as energy blasts struck the ground near his feet. He threw himself against the wall as another bolt flashed by, missing him, but striking one of the mute slaves square between the shoulder blades, and the man toppled to the ground. Unbelievably, the rest of the Walkers just continued with their work, unloading rubble into the furnaces as if nothing was happening, oblivious to the raging firefight that was going on around them.

'I thought Jackson ordered you to stay home,' Sam said, as he leant out and fired, knocking another Hunter out of the air.

'Lucky for you that I suck at following orders, then, isn't it?' Rachel said, grinning as she fired at the last remaining Hunter, winging it, but

137

not putting it out of action. It returned fire and multiple energy blasts slammed into the furnace that they were taking cover behind, tearing chunks out of the machine's heavy metal skin. A moment later, Nat ducked out from behind the furnace on the other side of the room and fired a three-round burst into the wounded creature, putting it down for good. As the last of the Hunters in the chamber hit the ground, Fletcher made a break for the door at the far end of the room, sprinting across open ground. Jay stepped out from cover, took careful aim at the fleeing man and fired. The bullet caught him high in his left arm, spinning him round and knocking him to the floor. Jay ran towards the fallen man with the others close behind him. As Jay approached, Fletcher struggled to his knees, trying to climb to his feet.

'Siddown,' Jay said, kicking him in the backside and sending him sprawling flat on his face in the dirt. Jay levelled his pistol at Fletcher as the man rolled on to his back and looked up at the four angry-looking children who now surrounded him.

'How's it feel?' Jay said, his voice shaking with anger. 'Knowing you're going to die.'

'You can kill me,' Fletcher said, clutching the bloody wound in his upper arm, 'but none of you are going to make it out of here alive.'

'Jay, no,' Sam said, putting his hand over his friend's gun and pushing it downwards until it pointed at the floor. 'We need him alive. He knows what the Voidborn are building here.'

'The what?' Rachel asked as they heard the angry buzz from outside of what sounded like a horribly large number of Hunters getting ever closer.

'The Voidborn, that's what the Threat call themselves,' Sam explained. 'That's what he told me, at least. We have to take him back to Stirling. The information he's got in his head could be invaluable.'

'Stirling,' Fletcher said, a frown appearing on his face. 'Iain Stirling? I might have known.'

'You know him?' Rachel said, looking confused.

'Oh, we're old friends,' Fletcher said with a pained laugh. 'And you're all his little helpers, are you? How amusing.'

'Shut up!' Jay barked at Fletcher. 'Sam, we can't take him back with us. You saw how he was controlling those Hunters—he'd bring every one of the Threat . . . or Voidborn, or whatever you say they're called now, right down on top of us.'

'Jay's right,' Rachel said. 'We can't risk them tracking us back to base. It's too risky.'

'Oh, do make your minds up,' Fletcher said. 'I'm not sure I can stomach much more of your indecisive whining.'

'That's it,' Jay said, raising his pistol. 'I'm finishing this treacherous piece of filth off.'

'Fine,' Sam said, turning and walking towards the exit, 'but make it quick.' It didn't matter what Fletcher had done, that he'd sold out his own species; something about killing another human didn't sit right with Sam. They'd all been changed by everything that had happened since the arrival of the Voidborn, but this was the one line that he could not bring himself to cross.

'Nothing personal, but you asked for this,' Jay said, pointing his pistol at Fletcher's head.

'You took the words right out of my mouth,' Fletcher said, closing his eyes.

A split second later one entire wall of the recycling chamber exploded in a flash of bright white light, knocking everyone in the room to the floor. Sam slowly dragged himself to his feet. It was almost impossible to see anything through the thick smoke that now hung in the air, but he felt something growling in his head and then the ground shuddered as a huge black shadow moved through the haze. Sam's fears were confirmed when the room was suddenly filled with a monstrous bellowing roar.

'Grendel,' Sam whispered to himself. A moment later a second roar answered the first from somewhere on the other side of the room. 'Oh, great,' he said, sneaking over to where Rachel and Nat were picking themselves up off the floor.

'We need to get out of here,' Sam said as the smoke in the room began to clear. 'Where's Jay?' He heard a groan from nearby and as the smoke continued to clear he saw Jay rolling over on to his back with a nasty gash on his forehead, blood trickling down the side of his face.

'Jay, you OK?' Sam whispered, helping his friend to his feet.

'Yeah, something hit me. Must have been a piece of debris or something,' he groaned, slowly standing up. 'Where's Fletcher?' He looked around for any sign of the man who had been right there just a few seconds earlier.

'Don't worry about him. We need to move,' Sam said, picking Jay's pistol up from the floor and handing it to him. A gentle breeze blew through the room and the smoke began to suddenly clear more quickly. A pair of Grendels, their heads almost touching the ceiling, were just fifteen

140

metres away on the other side of the room. One of the creatures turned its monstrous head towards Sam and the others, its huge mouth opening wide, razor-sharp teeth glistening as it spotted them and roared again.

'Run!' Sam yelled, and all four of them bolted for the exit. The two Grendels strode across the room towards them, the impact of their giant footsteps sending tremors through the floor. As Sam ran out into the crater compound, he saw that several of the outlying Voidborn structures were ablaze, with huge holes blown in their walls.

'We had to plant a few distraction charges on the way in,' Rachel said, sprinting along beside him.

'Don't worry, you made quite an entrance,' Sam said, looking over his shoulder as the two Grendels smashed their way through the doorway leading out of the recycling chamber. 'Your timing was impeccable. You might just have saved my juggling career.'

'Can we save the jokes for when we're not running for our lives?' Nat said, raising her rifle and fired a short burst at a Hunter that came buzzing out from behind one of the damaged structures, sending it spinning into the flames with an ear-piercing shriek.

'Where exactly are we going?' Jay asked as they ran headlong towards the crater wall.

'My plan extended about as far as running away from those things,' Sam said, jerking his thumb over his shoulder at the two giant, black monstrosities chasing them through the compound.

'You know, that's actually a good plan,' Nat said, glancing nervously over her shoulder.

'Don't know what you're worrying about,'

141

Rachel said, firing at another Hunter that came screaming towards them and sending it crashing to the floor. 'You've taken one of those things down before.'

'Yeah, I hate to remind you, Rach, but on that occasion there was only one of them and I had a rocket launcher,' Jay said when they reached the bottom of the crater wall. 'Biggest difference tonight? No rocket launcher.'

'Point,' Rachel said, and the four of them began to scramble up the steep crater wall. Behind them, the two Grendels pounded across the open ground between them and their prey, roaring in anger. As Sam and the others reached the top and hauled themselves over the edge, the Grendels were just reaching the bottom. The massive creatures began to climb, but their huge size made it more difficult for them because the loose soil and gravel gave way beneath their weight.

'Rach, wait,' Nat shouted as they sprinted towards the railings that surrounded the once magnificent park. She reached into Rachel's backpack and pulled out their last brick of plastic explosive. She ran back to the crater and placed the charge on the ground just above the climbing Grendels.

'Nat, you're a genius,' Jay said as she ran back to the others.

Rachel pulled the remote detonator from the pouch on her belt and waited as the first Grendel's massive claw reached up and over the edge of the crater, before slamming down on the ground and dragging the creature upwards. She hit the trigger just as the Grendel's head appeared, and the creature vanished with a bang in a cloud of fire and

142

dust. The burning, decapitated body of the Grendel tumbled back down the slope, knocking the other creature to the bottom of the crater.

'Bought us some time,' Nat said, 'but not much.' She pointed upwards and they saw half a dozen drop-ships racing towards them from the Voidborn Mothership. They climbed over the iron railings and on to the pavement. At the far end of the street another Grendel rounded the corner and roared as it caught sight of them.

'Other way I'm guessing,' Jay said, and they all sprinted in the opposite direction.

'Which route did you take to the surface?' Sam yelled at Rachel as they ran down the street with the Grendel striding after them, swiping aside the cars that sat in the road ahead of it like toys.

'Same way you did,' Rachel replied, 'We . . . erm . . . persuaded Adam to give us the route that he'd given to you guys.'

'Is that the closest entrance to the tunnel network?' Sam asked, trying hard to remember the map that Jackson had given him to memorise several weeks previously.

'I think so,' Jay replied as they ran round another corner, heading towards Big Ben, which was now just visible above the rooftops. 'The only other entrance that's sure to be open is Westminster Tube, but the entrance under Parliament is nearer and we know it's not blocked or locked up.'

'Well, we need to get undercover somehow,' Sam said, glancing over his shoulder at the descending drop-ships. 'If those things catch us in the open, it's all over.' He reckoned that they had a couple of minutes at best.

They kept running. The Grendel was now only

fifty or sixty metres behind them. Sam was very grateful that the roads were filled with abandoned cars in this part of the city because they were the only thing slowing the monstrous beast down. The street they were in at the moment was narrow enough to give them some cover from the drop-ships, but the approach to Parliament was horribly exposed. They had to move faster or they were going to be trapped between the Voidborn aircraft and the Grendel.

They reached Parliament Square just as the first of the drop-ships roared past, before banking and heading back towards them.

'Scatter!' Rachel yelled as the drop-ship began its run. They split up, all running in different directions, but still heading for the entrance to the Houses of Parliament.

The drop-ship opened fire, and massive green energy bolts struck the ground all around them, sending plumes of shattered tarmac and concrete shooting into the air. One blast hit a black cab just a couple of metres from Sam and the concussion from the blast sent him flying. He slammed on to the bonnet of another abandoned car and rolled off the other side, landing on his back on the road. He staggered to his feet, and ran as fast as he could towards the enormous Gothic Victorian building, praying that his three friends had not been caught by any of the blasts.

He was running in a zigzag pattern, just as he had been trained to do, when he heard another drop-ship screaming down towards them. This time none of the blasts hit quite so close to home, but the destruction they caused was no less devastating. Sam was surrounded by burning vehicles and the

144

black smoke that billowed from their blazing shells stung his eyes and irritated his lungs. He didn't mind; that very same smoke was probably stopping the Voidborn aircraft from drawing a more accurate bead on him. He was only fifty metres from the concrete barriers that had been put in place around the entrance to Parliament to prevent a terrorist from driving a truck bomb into the building. It suddenly seemed quite quaint to Sam that people had once been scared of other human beings, when the true threat would eventually prove to be something that humanity would be completely defenceless against. Regardless, he was glad that someone had once been so afraid of terrorists because those barriers now served as excellent cover. He vaulted over one of the massive concrete barricades and crouched down behind it as more energy blasts detonated all around the square. Sam lifted his head and peered over the top of the barrier. The smoke was so thick that the drop-ships had to be firing blind. Rachel and Nat were a few metres away; Nat was hobbling along, with her hand pressing down on a bloody wound in her thigh and her other arm round Rachel's shoulders. Sam jumped back over the barrier and ran towards them, putting his arm round Nat's waist and helping Rachel support her as they slowly made their way to the arched entrance to the Parliament buildings.

'What happened?' Sam asked, ducking involuntarily as another Voidborn aircraft screamed low over the square, presumably trying to spot a clear target.

'I took a piece of shrapnel in my leg,' Nat said, through gritted teeth. 'It's not as bad as it looks—I'll be fine.'

'Did either of you see where Jay went?' Sam asked, looking back over his shoulder into the smoke-filled square. There was no sign of his friend anywhere.

'No,' Rachel said. 'I haven't seen him since that first drop-ship made its attack run.'

'Will you guys be OK from here?' Sam asked as they walked beneath the archway and into the entrance area of Parliament.

'Yeah, I can probably get Nat down to the tunnels on my own,' Rachel said.

'OK, then, I'm going back for Jay,' Sam said, turning and heading outside.

'Sam,' Rachel said, and he turned towards her. 'Be careful.'

'Careful's my middle name,' Sam said. 'Actually it's not, it's Patrick, but you get the idea.'

She and Nat watched him vanish into the smoke.

The smoke outside was even thicker now, but for whatever reason the drop-ships had stopped firing, although Sam could still hear them flying around overhead. Suddenly, he heard a series of crunching thuds and he realised why the drop-ships had stopped their bombardment. Somewhere out there in the smoke there was at least one Grendel stomping around, presumably hunting for survivors. If Jay was alive, Sam had to find him before it did. He headed back past the concrete barriers and out on to the street. The only illumination was provided by the blazing wreckage that the drop-ships had left in their wake.

Sam crept along, the incessant low growl of the Grendel still inside his head. He closed his eyes for a second, trying to see if he could get an idea of where the massive creature was. It was no good; just like the sound that he heard from the Hunters, the noise seemed to come from everywhere at once. It varied in volume, but it gave him no sense of what direction the noise was coming from, only if it was moving closer or further away. He kept moving despite the intense heat from the fires around him.

Without warning the burning car a few metres to his right was suddenly hoisted into the air and hurled to one side, crashing into an abandoned bus and sending showers of flaming debris scattering in all directions. The Grendel roared at Sam and swiped at him with one of its huge claws. Sam dived to one side, feeling the breeze from the creature's talons as they slashed through the air just above him. He scrambled to his feet and sprinted away from the Grendel, expecting at any moment to be crushed by its talons.

'Look out!' Jay screamed, hitting Sam hard on the shoulder and sending him flying. A split second later another burning car flew over their heads and smashed into the front of one of the buildings that surrounded the square with an explosive crash.

'Come on,' Jay yelled, pulling Sam to his feet and pushing his friend back towards the entrance, to Parliament. As Sam ran headlong for the entrance, he could hear the pounding footsteps of the Grendel chasing after them.

Suddenly, he felt something wrap around his chest and squeeze, pulling him off his feet and dragging him backwards. Gasping for breath, he looked down at his chest and saw the oily black tentacle that was slowly tightening its grip as the Grendel reeled him in.

Jay ran towards the Grendel, raising his pistol and taking careful aim. He fired half a dozen rounds straight into the creature's face and it let out a howl of pain, raising a claw to one of its glowing red eyes where one of the bullets had struck home, half blinding it. The enraged creature took three long strides towards Jay and sent him flying with a backhand swipe of one of its claws.

Jay slammed into one of the concrete anti-terrorist barriers with a bone-crunching thud. Sam felt the tentacle round his chest release as the Grendel turned its attention to Jay who lay motionless on the ground. As Sam staggered to his feet, the creature raised one massive fist, preparing to crush Jay with a single blow.

'NO!' Sam screamed at the top of his voice as his skull was filled with a bizarre roaring sound.

The Grendel froze like a statue, its arm still raised. Sam stood there for a moment, gasping for air before a wave of searing pain hit him right between the eyes. It felt like a thousand needles were being pressed into his skull and he dropped to his knees, with his head in his hands, moaning. It lasted what seemed like an eternity but could only really have been a few seconds. He slowly got back to his feet as the pain subsided and walked towards Jay and the frozen Grendel. He cautiously walked around the Grendel, looking up at the creature, which was still active, its one good eye glowing, but was otherwise frozen in place. He turned his back to the Grendel, half expecting to feel its fist come smashing down on top of him.

'Jay, come on, talk to me,' Sam said, shaking his friend gently by the shoulder.

Jay groaned and his eyes fluttered open. 'I never

knew that everything could hurt at once,' Jay said as he pushed himself up into a sitting position.

'We need to get out of here,' Sam replied as the noise of an approaching drop-ship got louder, 'before those things start strafing us again. Can you walk?'

'Yeah, I think so,' Jay said, slowly getting to his feet with Sam's help. He looked up at the monstrous creature looming above them. 'What happened to that thing?'

'Just malfunctioned, I guess,' Sam said. He knew that wasn't true, that it had to be more than a coincidence that he had felt whatever it had been that had gone off inside his head a split second after the Grendel had frozen, but he wanted to talk to Stirling about it before anyone else, even Jay. He didn't know quite how his friends might react to the news that he seemed to have given the Grendel an order that it had for some reason obeyed.

'OK, that officially makes us the luckiest people on the planet right now,' Jay said, shaking his head. A moment later a drop-ship made a low pass over the square.

'Come on, time to go,' Sam said as they both saw the Voidborn aircraft banking back towards them above the Parliament buildings. They sprinted towards the entrance to the House, both feeling the last reserves of energy draining away from their battered bodies. The drop-ship opened fire, but the energy bolts missed their target as Sam and Jay ran for cover, striking the ground a dozen metres behind them. The two boys ran through the archway, taking the marble steps two at a time into the comparative safety of the famous building.

'This way,' Sam shouted, pointing down the

corridor that would take them back to the tunnel network. In the air above the building three more drop-ships banked sharply, the noses of the triangular aircraft turning towards their target. They fired indiscriminately, the massive bolts of green energy hammering into the building and blowing enormous chunks out of its structure. Inside, Sam and Jay struggled to stay on their feet as the whole building shook. Lumps of masonry fell from the ceiling and windows blew inwards in showers of glass shards.

'Keep moving,' Sam yelled. 'They're going to bring this whole place down on top of us.'

They ran down another dark corridor, the only illumination coming from the flashes of bright green light that accompanied the explosions outside. There was another green flash and the wall a few metres behind them exploded, filling the corridor with rubble.

'There!' Sam yelled, spotting the door that led to the stairs.

Outside the barrage continued, and the ancient building finally began to buckle under the assault. A volley of fire from two of the Voidborn aircraft slammed into the clock tower a third of the way up, and masonry that had withstood everything that had been thrown at it before finally gave way. With not a single human witness, the tower that had stood for one hundred and fifty years collapsed, and Big Ben fell, toppling into the very building that it had come to symbolise in a shower of shattered stone.

Sam and Jay reached the bottom of the stairs, blind in the darkness as they staggered into the tunnels, feeling their way along the walls. Above them there was a terrible groaning sound and then a noise like thunder. The stairwell they had descended a few seconds before vanished in a cloud of dust as it was filled with rubble from the destroyed building.

'Sam, are you OK?' Jay yelled.

'Yeah, I think so,' Sam shouted back.

At the far end of the tunnel a pair of torch beams came into view and Rachel and Nat walked towards them, Nat still leaning on Rachel for support due to her injured leg. They found Sam and Jay sitting with their backs against the wall of the rubble-filled tunnel, battered, bloodied and covered in masonry dust. Rachel looked at them both and a crooked smile appeared on her face.

'I thought Careful was your middle name?'

9

Sam and Rachel walked along the tunnel behind Jay and Nat. Jay had insisted on helping Nat despite the fact that Rachel had told him that she was more than capable of doing it. Sam had pretended not to notice the look of relief on Rachel's face when Jay had taken over. Sam turned round and briefly flashed his torch down the tunnel behind them.

'I think you can relax now,' Rachel said as Sam pointed the torch back ahead of them. 'I very much doubt that any of the Threat are going to be following us through that stairwell. It sounded like the whole building came down.'

'Yeah, I suppose you're right,' Sam said with

a sigh. 'Still jumpy, though, do you know what I mean?'

'Yeah, I'm always a bit twitchy after combat,' Rachel replied with a nod. 'It's quite normal, you know.'

'Do you think Nat's going to be OK?' Sam asked.

'I think so. It was a nasty wound, but I put a field dressing on it and that stopped the bleeding. It's nothing that Stirling won't be able to fix once we get back.'

Sam didn't reply, just nodded and was silent. In the light reflected from the torch, Rachel could see a worried frown on his face.

'Something's still bothering you, isn't it?' Rachel asked.

'Yeah,' Sam replied, his frown deepening. 'It's just that all this seems to have left us with far more questions than answers. I mean, you heard what Fletcher said. He obviously knew who Stirling was.'

'Yeah, the Doc's got a bit of explaining to do when we get back,' Rachel said with a nod. 'I just can't believe that someone would collaborate with the Threat like that.'

'The Voidborn,' Sam replied, 'that's what Fletcher said they were called.'

'Yeah, you said,' Rachel replied. 'I still think our name's more accurate.'

'He said some other things—seemed pretty crazy at the time, but . . .'

'Like what?'

'Well, he said that this has all been planned for a long time and that this planet has always belonged to the Voidborn. You don't think that could be true, do you?'

152

'No, I don't and frankly I would have thought you'd know better than to let a creep like that get under your skin.'

'Yeah,' Sam said, 'maybe you're right. But there's more to this than we know and Stirling hasn't told us everything he knows.'

'He's always been pretty secretive,' Rachel said. 'I wouldn't be that surprised if he does know more than he's letting on. It doesn't mean we can't trust him.'

'I suppose. I never expected there to be humans working with the Voidborn. It's just freaked me out a bit. I mean, how many people like Fletcher are out there?'

'Let's hope not too many,' Rachel said. 'Try not to worry about it. Just be glad that we all got out of there in one piece.'

'Yeah, you're right. It did look a bit hairy for a while.'

'I think that might be understating it just a bit.'

'Maybe a tiny bit,' Sam said, laughing.

Just ahead Nat's torch lit up the heavy steel doors that served as the underground entrance to their bunker. Nat leant against the wall while Jay banged three times on the door with his fist. A moment later the narrow panel set in the door at eye level opened and a pair of eyes appeared.

'Password?'

'Password is "Let us in, Jack, before I break your fingers", OK?' Jay replied.

'Well, when you put it like that,' Jack replied. A moment later they heard the sound of heavy bolts being drawn back and the door swung open.

'Welcome home.'

Stirling was absorbed in studying a computer-generated simulation of the waveform of the Voidborn control signal when his concentration was broken by a knock on the door of his quarters. With an irritated sigh he walked across the room and opened the door to find Anne standing outside.

'Jay, Rachel, Sam and Nat have just got back,' Anne said happily. 'They're in the Ops Area now. They look like they've been to hell and back. Nat's been wounded in the leg and they sent me to come and get you so that you could have a look at it.'

'OK, just let me save what I've been working on and I'll come straight down,' Stirling replied. He closed the door and headed back over to his terminal. He was just about to shut it down when an alert window popped up with a pinging sound. The small window read:

UNRECOGNISED TRANSMISSION SOURCE

Stirling frowned and opened up the custom-written signal analysing software and set it processing. He turned off the monitor and headed back towards the door. There was no point waiting; it usually took the triangulation equipment several hours to isolate the source of a new transmission somewhere in the city. Just as he put his hand on the door handle the terminal pinged again. He returned to the terminal with a frown on his face. There was no way that it could have completed the analysis that quickly. He switched the monitor back on and examined the results.

SIGNAL SOURCE LOCATED

Stirling read the coordinates listed below and felt his blood run cold. The signal was definitely alien in origin and the source was less than a hundred metres from where he was standing at that precise moment. He looked at the signal strength and felt a moment of panic. Whatever was sending that signal wasn't just telling the world its precise location—it was screaming it. He ran out of the room and down the corridor to his lab. He flew through the door at such a speed that he startled Will, who was sitting at one of the benches performing a secondary examination of a piece of the Hunter.

'Is everything OK, sir?' Will asked. He had never seen Stirling so panicked before.

'No, it isn't,' Stirling snapped. 'The signal tracker that Jacob took on the mission to Wembley the other night—where is it?'

'It's in the storeroom,' Will said, 'but why do you need it?'

Stirling didn't bother to reply; he simply ran through the lab to the storeroom door at the far end. He dashed into the cluttered room and desperately scanned the shelves for the object he needed. After thirty seconds he saw it and grabbed the small black box off the shelf and activated it. He punched in the wavelength characteristics of the signal he'd found and waited for several long seconds as the machine searched for it. A moment later the device pinged and the display indicated that it had a firm lock on the signal. The direction and range indicator confirmed Stirling's worst fears; it was coming from somewhere inside the base. He ran back through the lab and out into the corridor. He followed the arrow on the display indicating the direction of the source and realised that it was situated below his current location.

'Ops,' Stirling said under his breath, and sprinted through the double doors at the end of the corridor and flew down the stairs, taking them three at a time. He nearly sent Anne flying as he charged through the door into the Ops Area and saw Jackson standing off to one side as the other kids crowded around Sam, Jay, Nat and Rachel, peppering them with questions about what had happened on the operation that night.

Jackson looked over in surprise as Stirling ran towards them, his instincts telling him that something was very, very wrong the moment he saw the expression on his friend's face.

'What is it?' Jackson snapped as Stirling approached.

'Move,' Stirling shouted, pushing the others out of the way as he walked towards the four battered-looking members of the Ops Team. The regular beep that was coming from the device increased in frequency as he walked up to them one by one. As he moved towards Jay, the device began to beep faster and faster Stirling swept it up and down him, from head to toe.

'Turn round,' Stirling said.

'What's going on, Doc?' Jay asked, looking confused. 'What's wrong?'

'I said *turn round*!' Stirling barked.

'OK, OK,' Jay said, holding his hands up and

turning his back on Stirling.

Stirling swept the tracker down Jay's back and the beeping got faster and faster until he reached the empty ammo pouch hanging on the back of his belt. The beeps became a constant high-pitched tone and Stirling popped the pouch open and reached inside, pulling out a small black crystalline disc.

'What the hell is that?' Jay asked, looking over his shoulder.

'That is a Threat transmitter,' Stirling said, dropping the disc on the floor and stamping down on it hard. The squealing from the tracking device stopped immediately. Stirling looked at Jackson. He didn't need to say anything.

'Jack,' Jackson snapped. 'I want a rifle issued to everyone in the facility, NOW!'

'Everyone?' Jack asked. 'But . . .'

'I don't care if the nearest they've ever been to a real weapon is a water pistol,' Jackson barked at him, 'just do it!'

'Yes, sir,' Jack replied, running towards the armoury.

'What's going on?' Jay asked, sounding slightly bewildered.

'Fletcher,' Sam said, shaking his head. 'When the Grendels smashed into the Voidborn recycling centre and you got knocked out—he must have planted that thing on you, then.'

'What did you just say?' Stirling asked.

'Voidborn is what the Threat call themselves,' Sam explained.

'No, before that. Did you say "Fletcher"?' Stirling said, his eyes narrowing. 'Oliver Fletcher?'

'Yeah,' Sam replied, 'and he seemed to know

your name too.'

Stirling gave Jackson a fleeting glance that seemed to carry a lot more meaning for them than it did for the others.

'Right, well, we can all have a lovely little chat about this later,' Jackson said. 'Right now we have to assume that Threat forces are inbound to this location. I need everyone ready to fight.'

'Shouldn't we just run?' Rachel asked. 'We'll never be able to hold them off for ever.'

'We don't need to,' Jackson said. 'We just have to delay them while Doctor Stirling takes care of something. That much we *can* do.'

'How long have we got till they . . .' Sam fell silent, his question unfinished.

Through the heavy steel doors at the far end of the room they could all hear the sound of something approaching. Hunters. Lots of them.

Stirling ran into his quarters and over to his terminal. He launched the crash backup of the base's servers and watched impatiently as the machine calculated the time remaining. After a few seconds a message flashed up on the screen.

TIME REMAINING: 4M 38S

He ran back out of the room and into the lab where Will was still continuing his examination of the dead Hunter, clearly oblivious to what was happening downstairs.

'William, I need you to report to the Ops Area,'

Stirling said as he hurried towards the secure cabinet bolted to the far wall.

'What's going on?' Will asked, looking surprised.

'Our location has been compromised,' Stirling replied. 'Threat forces will be arriving any minute. I need you to go to Ops and help them hold the main entrance while I prepare for evacuation.'

Will just stared back at him, mouth hanging open.

'Now, please, William,' Stirling said punching the combination in to the keypad on the front of the secure cabinet.

'But I can't fight,' Will said. 'I've never fired a gun in my life.'

'William, if those things get past Ops before we're ready for evacuation, we're all dead,' Stirling said calmly. 'You can die up here or die down there, but at least that way you get to take a few of them with you.'

'Yes, of course,' Will replied, looking slightly dazed. He turned and walked out of the lab as Stirling opened the doors of the cabinet and pulled out the silver canister that contained their one real hope against the Voidborn. He placed the cylinder in a padded backpack, which he slung gently over his shoulders.

He hurried out of the lab, headed back to his quarters and checked the display on the terminal screen.

TIME REMAINING: 3M 27S

He opened a command console and began to type furiously. A few seconds later another window popped up with a password entry prompt. Stirling's fingers flew over the keyboard once more and a final window appeared.

FACILITY DESTRUCT SEQUENCE ACTIVE. REMOTE DETONATION PROTOCOLS ACTIVATED.

From somewhere below him he heard the sound of gunfire.

Jackson unfolded the bipod at the end of the barrel of the heavy machine gun and rested it on the sandbags of the firing-range wall, thirty metres from the main entrance door. He checked the belt of ammo that fed out of the box and into the gun, making sure that it would run smoothly and not get caught on anything. To his left, Rachel and Sam knelt behind the sandbag wall, checking the rifles that Jack had just issued to them and stacking spare magazines on the floor next to them within easy reach. Jay and Nat were on the other side of Jackson, doing exactly the same thing, with identical expressions of nervous concentration. Ten metres to the left of the firing range Jack, Kate and Adam took cover behind a pair of overturned metal cabinets, their weapons raised and ready. Twenty metres behind them Liz, Anne and Toby were crouched down behind three of the room's concrete support pillars, holding the rifles that they had just been issued with.

Behind them the door to the Ops Area flew open and Will ran in. Anne handed him the rifle that Jack had left for him, and he took it with the same expression that he might have used if someone had just passed him a live snake.

'Right,' Anne said, 'here's what Jack told me. The safety's off. Don't put your finger on the trigger until you want to shoot. We don't open fire till the Ops Team have fallen back behind us and then we just empty our rifles into anything that's moving. Once the ammo's gone, drop your gun and run. The Ops Team will cover our retreat upstairs. OK?'

Will nodded his agreement and crouched down behind one of the pillars, his face pale. Anne wondered if she looked just as terrified to him and decided that, yes, she probably did.

There was a sudden loud bang from the other end of the room and the heavy steel doors rattled as something hit them hard. Behind the sandbag wall, Sam pulled his rifle hard into his shoulder and his finger slipped inside the trigger guard, gently pressing the trigger. He sighted down the barrel of the gun, aiming at the dead centre of the left-hand door as it rattled again. Flashes of green light began to appear around the edges of the door as first one and then another Hunter energy blast hit it. The buzzing coming from the other side of the door was now a cacophony. He had never heard anything like it. The tunnel beyond had to be filled from floor to ceiling with Voidborn.

'Choose your targets, controlled bursts—I don't want any indiscriminate fire,' Jackson said calmly as the door started to groan and buckle under the sustained assault. 'Give 'em hell.'

The massive doors finally gave way, blowing inwards with a blinding green flash, and dozens of buzzing Hunters flew into the room. The Ops Team opened fire immediately, the roar of Jackson's heavy machine gun drowning out the other weapons as the first wave of attackers was cut down. The Hunters returned fire; sizzling bolts of green energy lanced through the air, blowing chunks out of the sandbags and the concrete walls as the Hunters laid down a blanket of suppressing fire.

'Keep firing!' Jackson yelled. 'Push them back!'

Sam tried to concentrate on individual targets, putting short bursts of fire into specific Hunters, but it was hard to track any individual target as the Hunters continued to swarm into the room.

'Reloading!' Rachel shouted as the magazine slid out of her rifle and clattered to the floor and she slapped a full one into place with the palm of her hand. The noise of gunfire, both human and alien, was deafening, and the smell of gunsmoke filled the air. The area around the door was now covered in the fallen bodies of countless Hunters, pools of dark green liquid surrounding them. But still they came. There was a sudden pained scream from Sam's left.

'Adam's hit,' Kate yelled.

Behind the Ops Team, Will saw Adam go down and immediately stood up, slung his rifle over his shoulder and ran for the first-aid kit that hung from a bracket on the wall nearby.

'What are you doing?' Anne yelled at him as he ran towards the fallen Ops Team member.

'What I've been trained for,' Will said, sprinting towards the locker from behind which Kate and Jack were still firing. He threw himself to the ground next to Adam and gently lifted the injured boy's hand from the wound in his shoulder. Adam groaned in pain.

'Let me see,' Will said. He examined the wound and quickly began to apply a field dressing. 'Don't worry, you're going to be fine.' Will secretly hoped that he was not making a promise he couldn't keep. The wound was bad and Adam was losing a lot of blood.

Sam felt like everything was going in slow motion. The sound of the gunfire was now just a continuous roaring in his ears, and inside his head he could hear the constant screeching hiss of the Hunters as they continued to pour through the door.

'I'm out!' Jay yelled.

'Fall back to the secondary position!' Jackson barked. 'Move!' The end of the ammunition belt fed through the machine gun and Jackson's gun finally fell silent too. He snatched up the assault rifle that was leaning against the sandbags and continued firing into the mass of silvery creatures as the Ops Team all began a fighting withdrawal towards the exit to the upper level of the base.

'Help me with him,' Will said to Jack, and the two of them carried Adam towards the rear of the room. Sam and Rachel stood shoulder to shoulder, slowly backing towards their secondary firing position, still shooting as they moved. An energy bolt streaked past, within millimetres of Rachel's head, and she hissed in pain.

'Are you hit?' Sam yelled over the sound of their rifles.

'Just a scratch,' Rachel said through gritted teeth. 'I'm fine.'

As the Ops Team passed the concrete supports,

Liz, Anne and Toby stepped out from their cover and opened fire. There was none of the Ops Team's trained precision, but their fire was still effective in its own way as they emptied their rifles' magazines into the advancing wave of Hunters. Sam and Rachel both grabbed fresh ammo from the cache on the table and reloaded while Jay and Nat returned to the secondary defensive line and began firing again.

'We're just slowing them down,' Jay shouted. 'I hope somebody's got a plan for how we're going to get out of here.'

'Hold the line,' Jackson said as he too opened fire. 'Just a couple more minutes should be all Stirling needs.'

Suddenly, Toby collapsed to the floor, a smoking hole in the centre of his chest. Will rushed over to him, but he did not need his medical training to know that there was nothing he could do for him. Will looked up at Liz and shook his head.

'Sam, Jay, stay here with me!' Jackson yelled. 'The rest of you upstairs NOW! Rachel, Nat, you go with them. You're their protection if we don't make it.'

'What about Toby?' Liz asked, tears in her eyes.

'Leave him,' Jackson said. 'He'll only slow us down.'

'We can't just . . .'

Without warning, the room was suddenly plunged into darkness, the only illumination coming from the muzzle flashes of the Ops Team's rifles and the glowing green energy bolts of the Voidborn forces.

'Stay calm!' Jackson shouted. 'They've taken out the generator. Backup batteries will kick in any second.' A few seconds later, just as he had promised, the lights on the walls flared back to life. 'Rachel, Nat, get the others upstairs!'

'Can you walk?' Will asked Adam.

'I think so,' he said with a pained grimace as Will helped him to his feet.

'Good,' Will said, taking Adam's good arm over his shoulders. 'Let's get you out of here.'

Jackson, Sam and Jay continued laying down a withering hail of fire on the Hunters, but now that they had successfully broken through the bottleneck kill zone at the door they were able to spread out across the room and take advantage of cover in exactly the same way the humans were. Still more of the Voidborn creatures were flooding into the room behind the first wave. There were now too great a number to count.

'There's too many of them,' Sam said, ducking back behind the concrete pillar as a volley of Hunter bolts slammed into it, blowing chunks out of the surface and exposing the metal rebar beneath.

'We slow them down for as long as we can,' Jackson said as he stepped out from behind another pillar and brought a couple of the closest Hunters down with two short bursts of fire. The Hunters had now advanced past the Armoury door, only ten metres from where Jackson, Sam and Jay were positioned. The Hunters' onslaught was now making it almost impossible for the last members of the Ops Team to return fire.

'Fall back!' Jackson shouted, pulling a smoke grenade from his combat harness and rolling it towards the approaching Hunters. The canister hissed and a billowing cloud of white smoke filled the room. Jackson, Sam and Jay took advantage of the cover the smoke provided and ran through the fire door behind them.

'You two, upstairs now,' Jackson said. 'I'm just going to organise a little surprise for our uninvited guests.' He reached into the large pocket on the thigh of his combat trousers and pulled out a block of C4. Sam and Jay scrambled up the stairs as Jackson planted the charge on the top of the door frame before following them upstairs. They found the others waiting in the corridor that led to the lounge. There was no sign of Stirling.

'Where's the Doc?' Jay said.

'Don't worry, Jacob,' Stirling said from behind him as he walked out of the corridor that led to the lab. 'I just had a few things to arrange.'

Suddenly, the floor shook and there was the sound of a massive explosion beneath them. Jackson came out of the stairwell in a cloud of smoke and ran down the corridor towards them all.

'I just brought half the stairwell down on their heads,' Jackson said. 'It'll slow them down, but not for long.'

'Good. I have everything we need. It's time that we left,' Stirling said. 'Get to the lounge, everyone. We'll be right behind you. Robert, I need to speak to you in the lab.'

Sam and the others sprinted down the corridor towards the main living area as Jackson followed Stirling to the lab. Once they were inside, Stirling turned to Jackson and let out a sigh. He took the pack off his back and handed it to his friend.

'That should be everything you need,' Stirling said. 'The weapon I've been working on is inside along with the drives containing the crash backup.'

166

'What are you talking about? Why are you giving these to me?' Jackson asked with a confused frown.

'Because I'm not coming with you,' Stirling replied. 'I have to stay here.'

'Don't be ridiculous—no one's staying here,' Jackson said, shaking his head.

'You don't understand,' Stirling said. 'The computers aren't working. I'd just finished the server backup when the Threat took out the generator. The emergency batteries only keep the lights working down here and if the facility's network isn't running there's no way to remotely detonate the self-destruct charges. If I had more time, I might be able to rig up some sort of timer delay for the detonation trigger, but . . .'

There was the sudden sound of Hunter energy weapons from below as the Voidborn forces began to blast their way through the rubble blocking the Ops Area door.

'We don't have any time,' Jackson said. He looked Stirling in the eye for a second and then, holding the pack out towards him, he shook his head. 'You're not staying, Iain, I am.'

'No, Robert,' Stirling said, refusing to take the pack. 'It's my mistake. I never considered the possibility that we'd need to trigger the self-destruct while we were running on backup power. It was a stupid oversight. I . . .'

'Iain, I'm just a grunt,' Jackson said. 'Those kids need you a lot more than they need me. I've taught them how to fight, but they don't know how to do everything that you can do. In this war, knowledge is power and you might be the only man on the planet who knows enough about those things up there to be able to give us all a fighting chance. We

167

can't afford to lose you. You take those kids and you get them the hell out of here. I'll make sure you're not followed.'

Stirling stared at his friend for several seconds and then hung his head with a sigh.

'Over here,' he said, beckoning for Jackson to follow him to a workbench that ran along the wall. An open breaker box was fixed to the wall above the counter and two wires led down from it to a car battery. One was already attached to one of the battery's terminals, but the other sat loose on the countertop.

'It's very simple,' Stirling said. 'Touch the wire to the positive terminal and . . . well . . . you know what happens.'

'Got it,' Jackson said. 'Now get out of here.'

Stirling turned to leave and then stopped.

'Robert, I'm . . .'

'I know, now go.'

Stirling slung the pack over his shoulder and walked quickly out of the room without looking back. He ran down the corridor to the lounge area and saw Sam and Jay standing on either side of the doorway with their weapons raised.

'Time to go, gentlemen,' Stirling said as he walked past them. He had a look on his face that suggested he was not in the mood for a discussion. He walked into the lounge area and saw Will applying another dressing to the wound in Adam's shoulder.

'Rachel, Kate, would you move that table out of the way, please,' Stirling said, gesturing to the large circular table that sat at one end of the room. The two girls lifted the table between them and moved it to one side of the room. Stirling walked over and pulled the worn-looking rug that had been under the table to one side. Underneath was a heavy metal hatch cover with a recessed keyhole in it. He lifted the hatch cover to reveal a ladder leading down a concrete tube that disappeared into darkness a few metres below.

'That's been there all this time?' Anne asked.

'Yes,' Stirling replied, 'and it's currently the only way out of here so if everyone could make their way down into the tunnel as quickly as possible it would be extremely helpful.'

'I'll go first,' Rachel said, switching on the torch that was attached to the underside of the barrel of her rifle and shining it down into the hatch. 'Just in case there's anything down there waiting for us.' She climbed down the ladder one-handed, her free hand aiming her gun into the darkness below.

Thirty seconds later, her voice came echoing back up through the escape hatch.

'All clear,' Rachel shouted. 'Come on down.'

Anne and Liz went down next, quickly followed by Kate and Jack. Stirling walked quickly over to where Will was finishing applying the new bandage to Adam's shoulder.

'How are you feeling?' Stirling asked.

'I've felt better,' Adam said, his face pale.

'I can imagine,' Stirling said. 'We have to leave. Do you think you can manage climbing down a fifteen-metre ladder?'

'I don't suppose I have much choice, do I?' Adam said with a pained smile.

'Not really, no,' Stirling said. He turned to Will. 'Have you given him any pain relief?'

'Yes, but only what was in that first-aid kit,' Will said. 'Really, he needs something more powerful,

169

but it's all I've got here.'

'I'll be fine,' Adam said, climbing slowly to his feet. 'Let's go.'

Stirling watched as Will helped Adam over to the hatch and down on to the ladder.

'We've got company!' Sam yelled from the door and a moment later there was the sound of gunfire. Stirling dashed over to the door, where Sam and Jay were both firing at the first few Hunters to have broken through the collapsed stairway, fifty metres down the main corridor.

'Both of you get down the escape hatch now!' Stirling barked over the sound of their rifles.

'What about Jackson!' Jay yelled. 'We can't just leave him behind.'

'He's made alternative arrangements,' Stirling said, frowning.

'What do you mean?' Sam shouted as he brought down another Hunter and then ducked back behind the door frame as several bolts of crackling green energy sizzled past.

'I don't have time to explain!' Stirling shouted. 'Now both of you get down that hatch!'

Neither of them had ever heard Stirling raise his voice in anger before and they both suddenly realised that Jackson wasn't coming with them. Jay gave a single nod, his face grim and the two boys turned and ran towards the hatch. Stirling followed immediately and they all hurriedly climbed through the hatch. He pulled it shut behind him and spun the wheel that locked the huge bolts on its underside in place.

'Get down into the tunnel quickly and go as far down it as you can,' Stirling said. From above him he heard the sound of something scraping at the

170

hatch and then a Hunter's energy weapon firing. The hatch shook and tiny particles of rust showered down on to Stirling's head. The hatch would not withstand that kind of punishment for long. Stirling realised with a sudden sadness that it wouldn't have to.

In the bunker's laboratory, Jackson sat on the bench next to the battery, staring at the exposed copper at the end of the wire he held in his hand. The first Hunter flew through the door and Jackson raised the pistol he was holding in his other hand and emptied the clip into the silver creature, sending it spinning backwards into the wall. Seconds later, two more Hunters burst through the door, turning towards him with a screech. Jackson dropped the empty pistol on the ground.

'Would've been nice to see the sky just one more time,' he said.

He pressed the end of the wire to the terminal.

Even a hundred metres down the tunnel below the facility the explosion was deafening. The tunnel shook and dust cascaded from the ceiling. There was a sound like thunder that lasted for several seconds as the facility was utterly destroyed and the building above it collapsed, burying it beneath thousands of tonnes of rubble.

'Thank you, Robert,' Stirling said under his breath. 'We'll make them pay, I swear.'

10

Stirling sat and listened in silence as Sam recounted exactly what he had seen inside the Voidborn facility beneath the Mothership. They had arrived at the safe house an hour earlier after a long, miserable walk along the escape tunnel and then a short but risky dash across an abandoned industrial complex in broad daylight. Stirling had led them down into one of the building's sub-basements and then through a hidden door into an area that was similar to the base they had just left, but on a much smaller scale. After the deaths of Jackson and Toby and the destruction of the place that had become their home, nobody had seemed to want to talk very much on the journey. Now Sam stood in the small room that Stirling had taken as an office as he sat behind his desk listening to Sam's report. The others were outside, busily trying to make the little space they now had to live in as comfortable as possible.

'And then we returned to base,' Sam said, completing his recounting of the previous night's events. 'Obviously we had no idea that the Voidborn had tracked us back there. I can't help but think that if we'd just—'

'Thank you, Sam. That will be all for now,' Stirling said, cutting him off. 'I'm going to need to think and plan our next move. I'll speak to you all in a while.'

'I'm not going anywhere until I get some answers,' Sam said. 'I want to know why Fletcher knew who you were and I want to know now. I've had enough of being kept in the dark. You know far more than you're telling, and if you expect us to do anything for you ever again you'd better explain what's going on right now.'

Stirling turned angrily to Sam; he stared at him in silence for a few seconds before his frown gradually softened. 'You really want to know?' he said, sitting back in his chair with a sigh. 'Well, I suppose you deserve that much after everything you've been through. I should warn you that some of what I'm about to tell you might be upsetting to you personally. Are you sure you want to hear it?'

'I'm sure,' Sam said. 'Tell me.'

'The simple answer is that once upon a time Fletcher and I were colleagues,' Stirling began, looking up at the ceiling. 'We worked for the same organisation, a group that calls itself the Foundation. Both Oliver and I were recruited by this organisation straight out of Oxford University. I was a biochemist and Oliver was a brilliant young computer scientist and a good friend. The offer the Foundation made us was one that would be impossible to resist for any young research scientist. Unlimited funding, limitless resources, the very best facilities and all the equipment that money could buy. There were only two conditions attached: we were never allowed to know where the technology or samples we were given to study came from, and we were not allowed to discuss our findings with anyone.

'Now, there are many young scientists who would say that it would be totally unacceptable to work under such conditions, that it goes against the fundamental scientific ideals of freely sharing knowledge. I wish I could say to you that that was how we felt, but it would be a lie. It's always disappointing, I suppose, what a man will do out of greed. It wasn't that we were greedy for the money, though it was exceptionally good; it was greed for more knowledge of the things we were being given to work on. It was more advanced than anything we had thought possible. Years, decades, even centuries ahead of its time. Biotechnology, nanotechnology, computer technology, you name it, we were given it.

'After we had worked for them for several years we were told that we had been selected for promotion within the Foundation and that as a result we would be told more about the source of the technology we had been researching. We had of course both discussed this before and I think we both had an inkling about what the truth might be. We were just reluctant to admit it, even to ourselves.'

'It was the Voidborn,' Sam said.

'Yes,' Stirling said with a nod, 'though we had no idea then that was what they were called. We were simply told that the technology was extraterrestrial in origin. They also told us that, if we wanted to truly become involved in communicating with these beings who provided the technology, we would need to have a device implanted in our heads that would allow us to communicate with them non-verbally. It seems hard to believe in hindsight, but both of us submitted to the procedure voluntarily, even eagerly—so blinded were we by our curiosity.'

'So you had spoken to the Voidborn before they arrived here on Earth,' Sam said, looking astonished, but still struggling to see how this had any bearing on him.

'The implants allowed them to communicate with us, but it was a one-way street,' Stirling replied. 'We were not permitted to initiate communication. They would contact us and then we would hear their thoughts in our head. We only spoke with the Voidborn on two occasions, but it was enough to convince both of us that they were real and that it was not just some elaborate conspiracy. The way they communicated with us was far beyond anything that anyone on this planet was capable of. It was the most bizarre sensation; feeling a thought and knowing that you did not create it, that it was an idea formed in an alien being's mind. It's hard to explain unless you've experienced it.

'However, there were clearly some members of the Foundation who were unhappy about the fact that, though we had all acquiesced to having these devices implanted inside our heads, no one really knew how they worked. They wanted to know how we might be able to construct and implant our own devices that would not transmit our thoughts to the Voidborn. I very much doubt that the Voidborn had any idea that Oliver and I were tasked with reverse engineering the implants, but as it turned out they need not have worried, at least initially. We were getting nowhere; the device was just too far ahead of anything that we had ever seen.

'That was when a third member was added to our team. His name was Daniel Shaw and he was a nano-engineer of unparalleled skill. He was younger than Oliver and myself, but he was cleverer than both of us put together. It is not often that one encounters true genius, but that's what

175

he was. It was humbling to work with him. Within weeks we had made more progress than we had in the previous two years. What we discovered was surprising at first and then it slowly became more disturbing. The devices were more than just a way to communicate; they were capable of changing, growing, developing. We had no way of knowing what they might become, but it was enough to make us suspicious of what the Voidborn were planning.

'Daniel developed a nanotechnological bug that would bond to the Voidborn implant without being detected and then retransmit any conversation that took place via that implant. In effect, it would allow us to eavesdrop on discussions we were not supposed to be privy to. The Foundation was arranged into cells, much like a terrorist organisation, so the only person who had any direct contact with the higher ranks of the group was our cell director. He would make periodic inspections of our lab, in order to review our work and ensure we were making progress. It was during the course of one of those inspections that we used a nano-injector to transfer one of the bugs into his bloodstream. One should always be wary of shaking hands with a nano-engineer,' Stirling said with a wry smile.

'And so you could listen in to everything the cell director was talking to the Voidborn about?' Sam asked.

'Yes, and within only a few days we heard the first reference to "the Plan" as they called it. It took us a while to work out what that meant, but suffice to say that "the Plan" is what you see unfolding on the surface now; the mass enslavement of humanity and the willing surrender of our planet to the Voidborn.'

'I don't understand,' Sam said, shaking his head. 'Why did the Voidborn need the Foundation's help at all? They took the planet without resistance anyway.'

'You're not seeing the big picture here, Sam,' Stirling said. 'The Foundation is not a few years old—it's not even centuries old—they've existed for *millenia*.'

'That's impossible!' Sam said. 'You're telling me that mankind has been in contact with the Voidborn for thousands of years and no one outside of the Foundation organisation has ever known anything about it?'

'That's exactly what I'm telling you,' Stirling replied. 'They've been silently guiding the path of humanity's development since prehistory, all on behalf of the Voidborn.'

Sam stared at Stirling with an expression of stunned disbelief.

'Never obviously, never ruling from on high, just manipulating our evolution from behind the scenes, artificially accelerating the pace of our development,' Stirling said, rubbing his forehead. 'That's how they operate. In recent times they have been the Foundation, but before that they went by other names. Numerous secret societies throughout history have merely been fronts for the activities of the Voidborn's representatives on Earth. Before that they were holy men or oracles who spoke to the gods, since the birth of human civilisation. We've been steered, controlled, for all that time, all at the will of the Voidborn.'

'But I still don't understand why the Voidborn

177

needed them to do it at all,' Sam said. 'What's the point of *accelerating* our development? Surely that just makes the planet harder to conquer?'

'They weren't worried about that,' Stirling said. 'I suspect they view us as little more than insects. To understand their reasoning you have to try to think like they do, which is almost impossible for us. We have no idea what the Voidborn look like physically, but I suspect they are a non-biological life form since they think of time in astronomical terms. To them, planning an event a thousand years, ten thousand years from now is the same as planning a year ahead for us. They have been preparing the Earth for their arrival for hundreds of thousands of years. For a species capable of interstellar travel these kinds of time spans become trivial. When they arrive, they want to find a large workforce that can be easily enslaved.'

Stirling stood up and started to pace back and forth in the tiny room.

'In 8000 BC there were estimated to be five million people alive on the planet,' Stirling said. 'Today there are seven billion. That's not just a phenomenal rate of growth, that's an *artificial* rate of growth. Without the Voidborn and the Foundation or one of its many predecessors influencing the course of our technological and social development that would have been impossible. They need that many people. They've been planning their arrival to coincide with the point in human history where population is at its current level. That point is now.'

'And now they're just going to use all those people to do what? Strip the whole planet of anything useful? They're like locusts,' Sam said.

178

'Why would anyone want to help them? What does the Foundation get out of this?'

'The usual things that lie behind any great act of evil: money, power, even ideology,' Stirling replied. 'For the men and women who serve them now, though, it's simpler than that.'

'Survival,' Sam said. 'At least, that's what Fletcher said.'

'Yes, that sounds like Oliver,' Stirling replied. 'He's always been good at surviving. When we found out what the Foundation was planning, at first we couldn't decide what to do. It seemed too big for us to do *anything* about. That was certainly what I felt, but Daniel was determined that we had to do something to try to stop them. Oliver didn't seem to be able to make up his mind—or that's what we thought at the time. Daniel persuaded us both that we had to try to convince someone in a position of power of the threat that we were all facing.

'His plan was simple; he would develop a nanobot that would block the transmissions from our implants so that the Foundation would not be able to track us down. Then we would go on the run with the most advanced pieces of Voidborn technology that we could get our hands on and hope that we could use them to convince someone in authority of our story. Daniel put the nanobots in us to block the transmissions from our implants, but he didn't activate them immediately. He waited, I think, because he was suspicious of what Oliver was going to do. He was always a better judge of character than me.

'Two days before we had planned to go on the run, Daniel turned up at my house and told me that

179

he had just overheard our section chief requesting permission to order our termination. Oliver had told them everything. Daniel had grabbed what Voidborn technology he could and fled the lab. That evening we both turned ourselves in to the British intelligence services and prayed that we had not made a mistake.'

'Did they believe you?' Sam asked. 'About the Voidborn, I mean?'

'Would you have done?' Stirling replied. 'I certainly wouldn't. The technology we'd brought with us was analysed and it raised enough eyebrows for us not to be just dismissed as lunatics, but no one believed us when we told them where the technology came from. Perhaps we'd spent so long knowing about the Voidborn that we'd forgotten that to anyone else what we were describing would just sound like the ramblings of mad men. They very much wanted to know where it *did* come from, though, as anyone with access to technology like that was clearly a threat to the defence of the realm. We were both kept in solitary confinement in a military prison for several months while they tried to work out what to do with us and their scientists tried in vain to reverse engineer the Voidborn technology. I suspect that we would have eventually been thrown to the wolves if it hadn't been for one thing. Inshore.'

'Who's Inshore?' Sam asked.

'Not who,' Stirling said, 'where. Inshore is a remote spot in the Scottish Highlands where a Voidborn scout vessel crashed. They sent a full platoon of marines to investigate the crash site and only two came back. As snipers, those two men were lucky enough to stay out of the range of the control signal that the damaged ship was transmitting. The rest of the platoon turned on each other and killed their own comrades for no apparent reason. The exact same thing happened with the second platoon that was sent in except that time there were no survivors, despite them all wearing full NBC protective suits.

'Eventually the RAF were called in and the entire site was carpet-bombed. There was enough left of the wreckage that the two crazy men talking about a race of mind-controlling aliens planning an invasion of Earth suddenly started being taken much more seriously. We were given carte blanche to spend as much as was necessary on finding a way of blocking the Voidborn mind-control. As far as we knew, the only way was to have a Voidborn implant in your head—everyone else was defenceless.

'The SAS raided the Foundation facility where Daniel and I had worked, but there was no trace of anyone or anything left there. They'd probably evacuated on the day we'd run, so by the time of the raid the trail was well and truly cold. We set to work immediately and we quickly realised that we would need an active implant that we could work with if we were going to make any real progress. Unfortunately, the only two we had were inside my and Daniel's heads.'

'I can see how that might have been a problem,' Sam said with a frown.

'I surgically removed Daniel's implant,' Stirling said. 'That left us with one intact working Voidborn implant with which we could experiment. We made several attempts to recreate it, and eventually we had a prototype that we felt would be capable of blocking the control signal without immediately transmitting its own location to the Foundation. That implant was largely our own creation, but parts of it were taken from Daniel's original implant. The first implant procedures with this prototype were not successful. There were a couple of fatalities and it was beginning to look like we would never be able to work out exactly how the Voidborn got the implants to bond successfully with the nervous system.

'Daniel and I spent five long, frustrating years working on the problem and eventually he made a breakthrough. He discovered that our version of the implant would not bond successfully with fully developed neural tissue. Instead, it needed to be implanted into freshly formed, undeveloped neural tissue. His rather controversial suggestion was that we try to put one of our new implants into a child, specifically a baby. I know, it sounds dreadful, but we were desperate. If we couldn't find a way to make these devices work, it would leave the whole of humanity vulnerable to the Voidborn. The incident at Inshore had shown us what that would mean. A suitable test subject was found, an orphan, and the procedure was carried out. Daniel was right. The implant bonded perfectly with the child's nervous system and we had what we needed—a base upon which we could build our future research. That's how we found you, Sam. Because you have one of these.'

Stirling turned his head and parted the hair on the back of his head to show Sam a small scar at the base of his skull.

'Oh my God,' Sam said, feeling a chill run down his spine as he reached up and touched the identical scar on the back of his own head. 'You mean—'

'There's a Voidborn implant in your skull too, Sam,' Stirling said.

'But this scar is from an implant that controls my epilepsy,' Sam said, shaking his head. 'It's not . . .'

'That's just what you were told,' Stirling said, interrupting him. 'You were the baby that received the Voidborn implant.'

'What are you talking about?' Sam said angrily. 'I'm not an orphan. My mum and dad are out there somewhere, wandering around as slaves of the Voidborn.'

'I warned you that this would be difficult for you to hear, Sam, but please let me explain. As you grew older, Daniel spent more and more time working with you and seeing if you were developing an ability to access the more sophisticated aspects of the implant's functionality. Obviously, we did not want you communicating with the Voidborn. In fact, our implant was supposed to avoid that possibility altogether, but we were still keen to see if you would, for example, be able to communicate with the implant that was still inside *my* head. Daniel grew very attached to you and he told us that he thought it was wrong that you should grow up within the confines of a research facility and that we should find you an adoptive family. A family where you could grow up normally, while still remaining under observation in case any unforeseen side effects should develop.'

'You're telling me that my mum and dad aren't my real parents?' Sam said, feeling a sudden sense of disorientation. 'That I'm adopted?'

'Yes, I'm afraid so,' Stirling said. 'Your mother

183

and father were going to discuss this with you when you were slightly older, but obviously the arrival of the Voidborn meant that they never had the chance.'

'So you knew them?' Sam asked. 'You knew my mum and dad?'

'Yes, of course,' Stirling said with a sad smile. 'When I went on the run from the Foundation I had to live under an assumed name. Our governmental handlers put us into a witness protection programme so that we could continue with our lives without constantly living in fear of the Foundation. I was James Taggart as far as anyone else in the world was concerned and Daniel . . .' Stirling paused, looking Sam in the eye. 'Daniel was Andrew Riley.'

'Oh my God,' Sam said quietly. 'My dad was Daniel Shaw?'

'Yes, he was,' Stirling said. 'And he loved you very much. He had met your mother not long after the event at Inshore and they had already had a daughter of their own.'

'Do you know who my real . . . my biological parents were?' Sam asked, feeling dizzy as he began to comprehend the consequences of what Stirling was telling him.

'No, we were never told and Daniel never asked,' Stirling said. 'I'm sorry.'

'So are the others like me?' Sam asked. 'Have they all got implants in their heads?'

'Yes, but theirs are not the same as yours,' Stirling said. 'Once we'd had the success with you in getting one of our implants to work, it made the job of improving on that design much simpler. We developed several new generations of implants that we could introduce into a person's nervous system without invasive procedures. Daniel developed nanotechnological solutions that meant the next generation of implants could build themselves inside a person's body without the need for surgery. All it required was an injection, and over the course of the next ten years we successfully placed working implants in nearly a hundred different test subjects. They were all children like you, but we were implanting the devices in older and older children, working our way towards a viable solution for the adult population.'

'And the parents of these children let you do this?' Sam asked.

'No, they never knew what we were doing,' Stirling said, looking uncomfortable. 'We implanted them during the course of routine surgeries, and then later during vaccinations, once Daniel had perfected the technique for nanotech construction of the implants within the body. Don't forget that we had the full backing of some of the darker elements of the government. You'd be amazed at what they will allow you to do in the name of national security.'

'So that's how you justify it to yourself?' Sam asked angrily. 'That this was all done for the greater good.'

'You have to remember how important this was,' Stirling replied. 'The plan, once we had successfully developed an implant that would work for everyone, was to place implant nano-seeds in the water supply and instantly and simultaneously make the entire population immune to Voidborn control.'

'But it didn't quite work out like that.'

'No, the Voidborn arrived,' Stirling said with a sigh. 'We always knew they might. It was a race against time to develop the solution before they did, but we were too slow. I was immune to the effects of the first control signal thanks to my implant. Daniel, your father, would not have been so lucky since his implant had been removed. At first, the only other people who I knew had escaped the signal's effects were the two marines who had survived the event at Inshore and gone on to be the heads of security for our research facility.'

'Jackson and Redmond,' Sam said, putting the pieces together.

'Yes. When the Voidborn arrived it was a Saturday morning. Jackson, Redmond and I were the only three people at the facility. Daniel and I had been working on an experimental system that he thought might be able to place a shield around a small area and effectively block any Voidborn control signal. He had installed it in the bunker beneath the facility, which had been designed to provide us with a secure, hidden workspace in the event of an invasion. The very same facility where we used to live. It was really just an experiment. It used huge amounts of power and was far from portable, but it protected Jackson and Redmond from the signal. At first, we were as shocked and horrified by what happened as anyone, but we knew that there should be others who had not been affected by the signal and that they would need our help. Nineteen of the children who had been successfully implanted with signal-jamming devices were out there, somewhere in London, almost certainly frightened and alone.'

'I know how that felt,' Sam said, remembering
186

the panic and fear he had felt when he saw what had happened to the people around him. 'Were we the only ones who weren't mind-wiped by the Voidborn?'

'It's impossible to say. There may have been people out there who had natural immunity of some kind, but we've never found anyone who wasn't affected who didn't have an implant. I immediately set to work trying to find our test subjects. I came up with a way to use the transmitters on the facility's roof as the centre of a passive scanning network that would search for the unique tracking signals that we had designed our implants to transmit.'

'So that you could keep tabs on us all?' Sam asked with an eyebrow raised.

'Actually, yes,' Stirling said. 'We knew that it might be difficult, if not impossible, to find you all if the Voidborn invaded without warning. It was a sensible precaution.'

'Or you could use it to track us down if any of us found out what you'd done to us and run away,' Sam said angrily.

'That wasn't the intention,' Stirling said, 'but I can see how it might appear that way. We knew that we had to try to find the children with implants as quickly as possible, and so Jackson and Redmond made the first of many trips to the surface to try to locate them. We had used the signal tracker to find half a dozen of the implanted children when disaster struck. We'd always known that it was possible that the Voidborn might transmit the control signal again at some point so it was risky for Jackson and Redmond to leave the shielded bunker, but what we didn't know was that the Voidborn drop-ships could transmit a control signal too. The signal is much weaker and has a more limited range, but is no less effective. Jackson and Redmond were conducting a search sweep when a drop-ship passed over Redmond's position and he was immediately enslaved.

'Thankfully, Jackson was sweeping another sector, but he found Redmond walking towards the centre of the city, his mind gone. He knew that he couldn't let Redmond fall into the hands of the Voidborn; he couldn't be sure that they might not extract the location of our bunker from him. He was forced to shoot and kill his best friend. I'm not sure he ever forgave himself; he certainly never returned to the surface.

'From then on he simply trained the most capable candidates from the implanted children we had rescued, and we sent them out instead to retrieve any other test subjects we located. As you know, you were the last one we found. You proved to be particularly elusive. I was desperate to find you—I owed Daniel that much. At the time I didn't understand why you were so hard to track. Now I think I do.'

'I spent most of my time underground, hiding in the sewers,' Sam explained. 'That's probably why I was hard to find.'

'No, that wasn't it,' Stirling said. 'Do you remember, a few weeks before the Voidborn arrived, you started to experience headaches?'

'Yeah, Mum and Dad took me for a scan,' Sam replied. 'They said it was just a precaution, that they needed to check there was nothing wrong with the implant that controlled my epilepsy. Which I now realise was all a lie.'

'Well, there *was* a reason for your headaches. The Voidborn components in your implant were starting to grow. We didn't understand why or how it was happening, but your father was deeply worried. He spent a week developing a new type of nanobot that would greatly inhibit the growth of any Voidborn technology. He wouldn't give me any details of exactly how they worked and I strongly advised him against using such an unproven and untested technology on you. The nano-bots were highly experimental and using them without much more rigorous testing was extremely risky, but he was desperate. If the growth had continued, it would almost certainly have caused you irreparable brain damage. At some point, and without my knowledge, he must have administered those nanites to you.

'When Rachel and Jacob first brought you to the bunker and you were fighting the effects of the Hunter sting, I ran blood tests on you. Your blood was swarming with the nanobots. They were fighting with the Hunter venom, which is itself made up of self-replicating nanites, and you were winning. I've been researching the nanites I found in your blood for the past couple of months now and I believe that I've come up with a way in which we can use them as a weapon against the Voidborn. Something that could make a real difference.'

'And these things are inside me right now?' Sam asked, looking down at his hands with a slightly bewildered expression on his face. After a couple of seconds he looked back up at Stirling and shook his head. 'I can't believe this—it's too much to take in. It's like my whole life has been a lie. Why are you telling me all this now?'

189

'Because someone has to know,' Stirling said. 'With Jackson dead, I'm the last person on Earth who knows what the Foundation did, how they handed the planet to the Voidborn.'

'But why tell me?' Sam asked. 'Why not tell the others?'

'Because you were the first, Sam. You gave me and Daniel hope that we could protect people from the Voidborn, maybe even beat them and . . . well . . . because you're right: you deserve answers, no matter how difficult it may be to give them to you. I'm tired of carrying around secrets. I feel like that's how I've spent my whole life.'

'You know I have to tell the others what you've just told me, don't you? They all deserve to know the truth.'

'You're right,' Stirling said with a nod. 'I know I should tell them, but it might be easier for them to hear it coming from you. Besides, as I said, I need time to think about our next move.'

Sam got up to leave, his head swimming with everything that Stirling had just told him. In the space of a few minutes, he felt like his life had been turned upside down yet again. More than that, he realised, he suddenly felt like a tiny, insignificant part of a conspiracy that was almost too big to comprehend. Halfway to the door, he stopped and turned towards Stirling.

'The Voidborn are going to win, aren't they?' Sam said, looking Stirling straight in the eye.

'Yes, probably,' Stirling replied, 'but that doesn't mean we have to make it easy for them.'

'I don't . . . I mean . . . I can't believe it,' Rachel said. Thirty seconds ago, Sam had finished telling the others what Stirling had just told him and she was the first to speak. The others stood or sat around the small central room of the safe house with expressions of disbelief, confusion and anger on their faces.

'He's known this all along and he's just telling us now?' Jay said angrily. 'They put these things inside us and you're telling us that our parents knew nothing about it?'

'That's what he told me,' Sam said. 'Don't forget, though, that if it wasn't for these implants we'd all be just like the rest of the Walkers. Personally, I'd take the implant over spending the rest of my life as a Voidborn slave.'

'Sam's right,' Kate said. 'It doesn't matter if what Stirling did was right or wrong—we have to concentrate on the future. We have to beat the Voidborn and we're not going to be able to do that if we start turning on one another.'

'I'm not saying that we shouldn't fight any more,' Jay said. 'I'm just saying that he should have told us.'

'Yes, Jacob, I should have.' They all turned to see Stirling standing in the doorway of his room; he looked older and more tired. 'That was my mistake and if it's any consolation to you at all I regret not telling you sooner. Jackson always told me that I should have and he was right. What I won't apologise for, and you may not want to hear this, is what we did to you to make you immune to Voidborn control. You may question the ethics of it, but if we had not done what we did, there

191

would be no hope for us now. As it is, we are quite possibly the last form of concerted resistance to the Voidborn anywhere on the planet.'

'Why didn't you just tell everyone, the whole planet, what was going to happen?' Rachel asked. 'We might have had time to prepare, to defend ourselves.'

'Who would have believed us?' Stirling asked. 'And, even if they had, it would probably just have caused mass panic and we still had no means of protecting the adult population from Voidborn enslavement. It would have served no purpose.'

'That wasn't your decision to make!' Jay snapped. 'That's what this is all about—you like playing God, don't you?'

'Enough!' Sam yelled. 'I know you're angry, Jay. I'm angry. We're *all* angry, but we have a job to do. We can shout and scream at each other all we want, but it doesn't change the fact that there's a three-kilometre-wide Voidborn ship hovering over central London. It doesn't change the fact that we've all lost people we care about and it certainly doesn't get us our damn planet back. Only one thing can do that—us. Living together, working together, fighting together. If we can't do that, it's already over—the Voidborn have already won.'

Jay stared at Sam for a moment, still furious, and then after a couple of seconds he threw up his hands in surrender.

'OK, OK, you're right,' Jay said, sitting back down. 'So where do we hit them? 'Cos I don't know about anyone else, but I'm ready for some payback.'

'I think we all are,' Nat said. 'They hit us; now we should hit them right back, twice as hard. That's what Jackson would have done.'

'Indeed he would have,' Stirling said with a nod, a sudden look of cold determination on his face. 'And that's exactly what we're going to do.' He reached down and pulled a foot-long silver tube from the pack on the floor.

'What is that?' Will asked.

'This is what we're going to use to take the fight to the Voidborn,' Stirling said, placing the cylinder on the table at the front of the room. 'This cylinder contains a swarm of self-replicating nanites that will infect and corrupt any Voidborn technology that they come into contact with. In simple terms, it's a technological virus. It is my belief, based on the description that Sam provided, that, if we can successfully release the nano-virus into the machine that he discovered beneath the Voidborn Mothership, it will disable it permanently. I am not entirely sure what purpose it serves, but I think it's safe to assume, given the scale of the Voidborn's efforts to construct it, that it has to be rendered inoperative, permanently. What's more, any Voidborn technology that comes into contact with the machine will, in turn, become infected with the nano-virus. Any attempt to repair the machine or even approach the facility will simply result in more Voidborn becoming infected.'

'So we're releasing a Voidborn plague,' Anne said, eyeing the cylinder slightly warily. 'You're certain that this nano-virus isn't harmful to humans, that it won't spread unchecked?'

'I can be reasonably sure that it won't harm humans since it came from a human.' Stirling gestured towards Sam, who looked slightly uncomfortable. 'It will only spread into Voidborn technology. If this works as I think it will, we will transform central London into a viral hot zone that is a no-go area for the Voidborn for the foreseeable future.'

'Are you saying that we've got to go back to the Voidborn compound?' Nat asked. 'Because I hate to sound negative, but the last time we went in there we barely made it out alive and they're bound to have increased security after that. Couldn't we just release the virus somewhere nearby and let it spread naturally?'

'No,' Stirling replied, shaking his head, 'we can't give the Voidborn the opportunity to put any sort of quarantine in place. As I said before, I'm not entirely sure what that machine does, but I have a theory, and if I'm correct the machine is our priority target.'

'Why? What do you think it is?' Liz asked.

'Part of the Voidborn endgame,' Stirling replied, 'and very, very bad news for every living thing on the planet.'

'Sounds like a suicide mission,' Jay said, 'so, obviously, you can count me in.'

'I had a feeling that might be the case,' Stirling said with a tiny smile. 'Any other volunteers?'

'I'm in,' Sam said with a nod.

'And me,' Rachel replied.

'Well, you're not doing this without me,' Nat said.

'No,' Stirling said. 'I'm sorry, Natalie, but you're injured. I appreciate your dedication, but you're not ready for a mission like this yet.'

For a moment it seemed as though she was going to argue with him, but then she just sat back in her chair, looking irritated. The trip to the safe house had been difficult enough with her injured leg; much as she may not have wanted to admit it, she knew she wasn't ready for a mission like this yet.

'I'll go,' Kate said. 'Adam would never let me live it down if I didn't.'

'And you're going to need someone who knows one end of a gun from the other,' Jack said with a grin.

'I will also be accompanying you on this mission,' Stirling said.

'I'm not sure that's a good—' Sam said.

'I'm not going to argue about this with you,' Stirling said, cutting him off. 'This weapon needs to be deployed in the right location to ensure that the Voidborn machine is permanently and irrevocably disabled. I'm the only person who can be certain of doing that correctly. So I'm coming with you.' He looked around the room. 'William, Elizabeth, Natalie, Anne and Adam shall remain here and hold the fort. The rest of you need to be ready to leave at nightfall. We can't use the same route into the area that Sam and Jacob did yesterday so we will need to work out a new approach.' Stirling looked at his watch. 'We have three hours to put a plan of attack together. I suggest we get to work.'

11

The squad moved from cover to cover, trying to make as little noise as possible. Nat's prediction had unfortunately proved to be quite correct. There seemed to be a far greater concentration of Voidborn than when Sam and Jay had first scouted out the area the previous evening. They spent most of their time hiding, waiting for gaps in the Hunter and Grendel patrols, and progress towards their objective was, at times, frustratingly slow.

'Looks like you guys did a really good job of irritating them yesterday,' Jack whispered as the six of them hid in the darkened front room of an abandoned basement flat. He watched through a tiny gap in the lace curtains as another group of Hunters floated past outside.

'That's why we're going to need a diversion,' Sam said.

'I'm starting to wonder if that's going to be enough,' Kate said. 'I mean, I know that Jack's really good at blowing stuff up, but there's so many of them. Do you really think that we're going to get anywhere near the compound, even if they are distracted?'

'We're making progress,' Rachel said. 'It's not far to the compound's outer perimeter. Once we get there we'll have a better sense of what we're up against. If Jack's pyrotechnics can distract enough of the sentries and we manage to mingle with the slaves, we've got a chance. If push comes to shove, we'll just release the virus as close as we can to the centre of the compound and hope that it spreads quickly enough. Right, Doctor Stirling?'

'Yes,' Stirling replied. 'The nanite swarm should spread aggressively to any Voidborn that come within a few metres of a host. It's not an ideal solution, but it would be better than nothing. It may even be that under those circumstances the resultant chaos would give us an opportunity to enter the structure at the centre of the Voidborn compound and directly sabotage the machine within somehow.' Stirling had the cylinder containing the nanite dispersal device in the padded backpack that was hanging between his shoulder blades.

'That's assuming we ever get out of this flat,' Jack said. They all heard the thudding footsteps of a Grendel getting closer and the rumble of a drop-ship somewhere overhead. Sam heard the low growl of the Voidborn creature in the back of his head and noticed something strange about it. There was a higher-pitched whispering tone mixed in with the low guttural sound that the Grendels usually made. It was just like a sound he'd heard the previous night.

'Jack!' Sam whispered urgently. 'Get back from that window.'

Jack just had time to turn his head towards Sam, a slightly confused expression on his face, when a Grendel's tentacle smashed through the window behind him and wrapped itself round his neck. Jack gave a strangled cry of surprise and then he was jerked backwards and lifted through the shattered remains of the window and out of sight. The others backed away, raising their weapons, waiting for the next attack. Suddenly, a familiar voice came from the street outside.

'I know you're in there,' Oliver Fletcher said calmly. 'Your friend here appears to be having quite a lot of trouble breathing, so I suggest you throw down your weapons, come outside and surrender yourselves to me as quickly as possible. I really am so very keen to meet you all.'

'What do we do?' Rachel whispered.

'We surrender—what else can we do?' Stirling said with a sigh. 'Damn it all, how did he find us?'

'I'm not just giving up,' Jay said. 'I say we go down fighting.'

'He's got a point,' Kate said, her rifle still levelled at the window. 'We're dead either way.'

'No,' Sam said, dropping his rifle on the floor. 'Surrendering is not the same thing as giving up. Jackson taught me that.'

'He's right,' Rachel said, lowering her rifle and following Sam and Stirling towards the door.

'Guess this really was a suicide mission,' Jay said as he watched Kate slowly lower her weapon.

Sam walked up the stairs from the flat's front door and out on to the street. Fletcher stood in front of the Grendel with a triumphant smile on his face. Jack hung a metre off the ground, his hands clawing at the slick black tentacle wrapped tightly round his throat. Fletcher turned to the Grendel, closing his eyes for a split second and the giant creature lowered Jack to the ground and released him. Jack collapsed to his knees, sucking in ragged lungfuls of air. There were drop-ships hovering at either end of the street and half a dozen Hunters were approaching from each direction. Sam heard the persistent buzz of the Hunters in his head, but once again it was layered with the strange whispering he had heard before. Obviously all these creatures were under Fletcher's control, all thanks to his Voidborn implant. Sam tried to concentrate as Kate and Jay came out of the flat, hands raised. Sam tried desperately to exert control over the Grendel as he had done the previous evening, but it was no good—he couldn't give the giant creature an instruction. He still had no idea how he'd managed to do it before. The Hunters descended on the

198

captured Ops Team, tentacles wrapping round their arms and holding them in place.

'How lovely to see you again, Iain,' Fletcher said as he walked up to Stirling. 'We've been looking for you for *such* a long time. I know someone who is very keen to talk to you. I'm afraid you're going to find out the hard way what happens to people who betray the Voidborn.'

'Wake me up when the monologue's over,' Stirling said calmly. 'You always did like the sound of your own voice, Oliver.'

Fletcher closed his eyes for an instant and Stirling gasped in pain as the Hunters holding him tightened their grip, crushing his arms.

'And you're still as naive as I remember you,' Fletcher said, his voice dripping with contempt. 'And here's our little Trojan Horse,' he continued, standing in front of Sam.

'I don't know what you're talking about,' Sam said.

'Oh, if it weren't for you it would have been much harder to find everyone. You see, now I know all about your little passenger up here.' He tapped the side of Sam's head. 'I have done ever since you did this.' He pulled a crystal disc from the pocket of his overcoat and held it in the palm of his hand. A moment later a video was projected into the air above the disc. It appeared to have been shot by a camera on-board one of the drop-ships that had been flying over Parliament Square the previous evening. It showed Sam shouting at the Grendel that was about to crush Jay to a pulp and the monster being frozen in its tracks.

'You see, you're not supposed to be able to do that,' Fletcher said, 'not unless you have a

Voidborn interface implant and only members of the Foundation have those. So once we saw this footage we ran a scan for any implant that had started transmitting within the past twenty-four hours and, lo and behold, there you were, sneaking back towards our compound.'

'That's impossible,' Stirling said. 'His implant can't transmit.'

'Oh, Iain, you're really nowhere near as clever as you think you are, you know,' Fletcher said with a nasty smile. 'The boy's implant started to transmit the instant he used it to exert control over one of these things.' He gestured over his shoulder at the Grendel. 'You can't have it both ways; the moment he used it, the Voidborn could detect him. They only had to realise that and start looking.'

'Wait a minute,' Sam said. 'What do you mean "one of their machines"? You mean these aren't Voidborn?'

'Of course not,' Fletcher said, laughing. 'Does this hulking brute really look like something that could enslave a planet? These are just the Voidborn's tools, constructs that do their dirty work. The machines you call Hunters, the Voidborn call Workers, and these,' he said, pointing at the Grendel, 'are Soldiers. Don't worry, though; ever since your little trick with one of the Soldiers last night the Voidborn have been very keen to speak to you. You'll be meeting them soon enough, though I have to tell you that I don't think you're going to enjoy the experience.'

Fletcher walked further along the line of prisoners, looking at Jay, Rachel, Kate and Jack.

'You shouldn't all look so worried,' Fletcher said, smiling at them. 'There's really nothing to

200

worry about. Well, other than whether or not the Voidborn bother with an anaesthetic before they dissect you, of course.'

'At least I'm not a traitor to my whole species,' Jay said angrily.

Fletcher closed his eyes and Jay gasped in pain as the Hunter holding him snapped his wrist effortlessly.

'I can do that all day,' Fletcher hissed, bringing his face close to Jay's. 'Anything else you'd like to say?'

Jay opened his mouth to say something.

'Jay, don't,' Rachel said. 'Don't give him the satisfaction.'

He closed his mouth, his jaw muscles clenched, fighting to ignore the waves of pain shooting up his arm from his broken wrist.

'Your friend here is clearly a lot cleverer than you, young man. You'd do well to listen to her,' Fletcher said. 'Well, we can't just sit around here all night—we have people to see.' He closed his eyes for a moment and the Hunters started marching them towards the Voidborn drop-ship that was slowly descending towards the ground at the far end of the street. As it touched down, a hatch in the side opened up and a wide ramp was lowered. One by one the Ops Team were escorted up the ramp by the Hunters and into the belly of the Voidborn aircraft.

Sam didn't bother struggling against the Hunters' hold on his arms; he knew from the previous night that it would be pointless. They pushed him through the hatch and he got his first look at the inside of the drop-ship. The floor looked like it was made of black glass covered

201

with spiderweb cracks that pulsed with green light. The walls were made of the same material, but they were covered in irregular cuboid blocks that pulsed with an identical eerie glow. The air inside was uncomfortably hot and dry and Sam could hear another background noise in his head, a kind of squawking chatter interspersed with digital distortion. The Hunters pushed him down next to Rachel and held him firmly in place. Jay grunted in pain as the Hunters shoved him next to Sam, with no regard for his shattered wrist.

'I've got a horrible feeling we're not getting out of this one,' Jay said quietly.

'We're not dead yet,' Rachel replied.

'Oh, we're not out of this yet,' Sam whispered. 'Don't worry about that.'

Stirling was still wearing his backpack.

Sam felt an impact run through the floor of the Voidborn drop-ship as it touched down. He guessed they had been in the air for only five minutes or so and that meant there was only really one place they could be. The Mothership. The hatch at the other end of the compartment opened silently and Fletcher stepped outside. The Hunters holding the prisoners hauled them to their feet and shoved them forward. Sam had spent most of the short journey trying to will either of the Hunters holding him to release their grip, with no success. Whatever it was that he'd done to the Grendel the previous night, he did not seem to be able to repeat it. It seemed unfair to him that the ability that had

202

started his implant transmitting and so given away the Ops Team's location was now not working when he most needed it.

The Hunters pulled him through the hatch and down the ramp, and Sam's mouth fell open in amazement at the sight before him. He was in an enormous hangar, its walls covered in the same black glass cuboids that had lined the interior of the drop-ship. One end of the giant space was open but covered by a glowing green energy field, and all around them dozens of drop-ships were neatly lined up with Hunters swarming around them, apparently performing routine maintenance. Above them, hundreds more drop-ships hung from the ceiling, noses pointing downwards, looking almost like bats nesting on a cave roof. Recessed alcoves lined the walls and docked within each of them was a Grendel. There was no sign of life from any of the monstrous creatures, but it was still an intimidating display of power. The walls and floors all pulsed with green light, which seemed to converge and pool around the drop-ships and the Grendels; there was no way of knowing what the light did, whether it was transmitting power or data, or something else entirely that was beyond his comprehension.

What was most overwhelming was the sheer scale of everything. The Ops Team suddenly seemed very small and insignificant by comparison, and for the first time Sam felt a twinge of despair. He had a dreadful feeling that all of their struggle had been for nothing, that they'd just been throwing pebbles at a tank, thinking they could slow it down or even stop it. Their bravado seemed arrogant, foolish even.

'I don't think we're in Kansas any more,' Rachel said as the Hunters pushed them down the ramp and on to the floor of the hangar.

'Yeah, it's quite something,' Jack said. 'This is just one of the Motherships, though. The TV reports when these things first arrived said they were showing up all over the planet. Just think how much hardware there must be on all of these things put together.'

'It's weird,' Sam said to Jay as they were pushed across the hangar. 'It's like they were expecting a fight.'

'What's weird about that?' Jay asked, wincing as the Hunters jarred his wrist again.

'Well, the control signal is supposed to enslave everyone, right?' Sam replied. 'So, if they're expecting little or no resistance, why bring an army?'

'We'll have to ask them when we meet them,' Rachel said.

'Assuming they're not too busy with the whole dissection thing, that is,' Kate said with a grim smile.

Fletcher walked several metres ahead of the Ops Team, with Stirling being pushed along beside him.

'Are you starting to realise how pointless it's been to oppose this?' Fletcher asked. 'How insignificant we are in comparison to them? You could have joined the Voidborn too, Iain, had a future among the stars. Instead you threw it all away in a pointless act of resistance.'

'Jacob was right, Oliver. You're a traitor to your species, to the whole planet,' Stirling replied. 'Have you stopped and looked at what's happening down there? What they're doing to humanity? How can you be a part of that?'

'I'm afraid that humanity's days are numbered, Iain, and I've never been one to back a loser.'

'No, you're much too clever for that, aren't you?'

'Oh, I think you're the clever one, Iain, figuring out a way to block the control signal without using an implant we can detect,' Fletcher said. 'I'm going to enjoy working out how you did it once we've finished analysing these children's corpses.'

'I can't decide whether you disgust me or if I pity you, Oliver,' Stirling said, shaking his head.

'Well, we'll see if you still feel so superior after you've met the Voidborn face to face. I think you're probably due a lesson in humility.'

They were all marched out of the hangar and down a long corridor that started to spiral slowly upwards, opening up on one side to reveal a stream of sparkling green energy encased in an enormous crystalline column that rose hundreds of metres above them. It emitted a low throbbing hum that echoed the pulsing of the waves of light through the black cubes on the wall. The more Sam saw of the interior of the Mothership, the more it felt like being inside a living, but non-organic creature. They continued the long walk upwards. Hunters floated past occasionally or could be seen with their tentacles embedded in the walls, patterns of green light dancing across their silver skins. As they neared the top of their climb, Sam finally saw what was at the top of the crystal column. In the centre of the ceiling at the top of the shaft that the corridor encircled was a giant black crystal, the size of a house. The energy stream from the column struck the crystal, creating a white-green light that was almost too intense to look at. The energy crackled across the surface of the crystal and then radiated outwards across the ceiling in all directions until it struck a glowing ring at the outermost edges. Despite the obvious danger they were in and everything that he had been through in the past couple of days, Sam found it strangely beautiful. They finally stopped at a huge black slab covered with elaborate carvings of sweeping elliptical patterns.

'You are honoured,' Fletcher said. 'Very few humans have ever had the privilege to meet the Voidborn.'

Fletcher walked up to the slab and placed one hand on the warm surface, and fine lines of green light began to race along the engravings, converging beneath his hand in a glowing pool. A moment later the slab began to split apart, huge triangular sections receding into the walls and opening the way into a chamber beyond. The room was semicircular, with the curving wall and floor made up of transparent panels that offered a startling view of the darkened city beneath them. At the centre of the shadowy sprawl, far below, was the glowing shape of the Voidborn compound, slowly expanding, consuming the heart of the city. On the opposite wall of the chamber was a three-metre-tall black cylinder with thick bunches of glistening techno-organic cables sprouting from its base and trailing away into the darkness below. The pit beneath the cylinder appeared to be bottomless, only the occasional flashes of green light that ran up its walls giving any sense of how far down it went. Half a dozen Hunters floated in the air above the edge of the pit, standing silent guard. Sam noticed that they were different to the normal

Hunters. They were significantly larger and their carapaces were jet-black. As the Hunters pushed them all towards the pit, a narrow walkway slid out with a hiss, extending from its edge towards the black column. Fletcher walked on to the walkway, approaching the cylinder.

'These are the humans that were responsible for the attack on the facility last night,' Fletcher said, apparently talking to the air. 'As you requested, I present them to you for further examination.'

A moment later, the surface of the cylinder, which had seemed solid just a moment before, began to ripple and shift, almost like a liquid. As the Ops Team watched, the cylinder seemed to explode in a shower of dust, but the dust did not simply fly in all directions; it began to flow and coalesce into a distinct shape. As they watched, the swirling black cloud formed itself into a humanoid form—a woman with skin like highly polished black glass. Her eyes glowed with green light and wisps of black vapour, the remains of the dust cloud, trailed in her wake. Fletcher backed away from her as she made her way across the walkway towards the Ops Team. The Hunters forced Sam to his knees and he felt a strange sense of almost animal panic as the gleaming obsidian woman approached.

'We are Voidborn,' the woman said as she walked up to Stirling. 'You are known to us. Human designate Stirling, traitor to our kind. We are pleased you have been found. You were dangerous to us perhaps, but no more.'

She walked past Stirling and towards Sam.

'You are not known to us,' the Voidborn said, 'but we sense our technology within you. The technology was once part of Human designate

Shaw, another we seek. We shall remove the technology and it will tell us his location; he shall not remain lost to us.' She stopped for a moment and looked at Sam, as if examining him. Sam felt a sudden horrible sensation and somehow he instantly knew it was the Voidborn forcing her way inside his head, pushing into his mind, scratching at the inside of his skull.

'You have a weapon,' the Voidborn said, tipping her head to one side, her eyes narrowing. 'No.' She pointed at Stirling. 'He has a weapon. Something that may harm us.' She walked behind Stirling, who struggled fruitlessly against the Hunters restraining him. She stretched out the fingers of one hand and her fingertips extended, stretching into long curved blades. She raised her hand and slashed it downwards, tearing a jagged hole in the material of the pack on Stirling's pack. She reached inside and pulled out the silver cylinder containing the weaponised nanites. The Voidborn examined the cylinder and frowned. 'This device swarms with life, but it is not Voidborn, nor is it human.' She walked round Stirling, turning to face him. 'Tell me, human designate Stirling, what is this?'

'Why don't you open it and find out?' Stirling said.

'No, we shall analyse it remotely, safely. We were incorrect; you are still dangerous to us. The threat will be eliminated. Easier if you tell us the contents, explain the new life you have created; but you are known to us, you will resist. We also suspect that there are more of your young who are not controlled by us. We would know where they hide.'

'I'll tell you nothing,' Stirling said defiantly.

'Then perhaps I shall pluck the knowledge from this one's head,' the Voidborn said, pointing at Sam. The Voidborn handed the cylinder to one of the black Hunters before walking up to Sam and placing one cold glass hand on his cheek. 'Let us see what else you can tell me.' Again Sam felt the hideous sensation of the Voidborn's mind slipping into his. He felt a moment of powerless despair and then suddenly it seemed as if something had exploded inside his head. It wasn't painful, just overwhelming, like a rush of awareness or a moment of complete understanding. A single drop of blood trickled out of his nose. The Voidborn instantly recoiled from him as if she had been burnt, hissing with hate, her eyes narrowing.

'What did they do to you?' the Voidborn said angrily, staring at Sam with something that almost looked like fear. She strode over to Stirling and clamped one smooth hand round his throat. 'What did you put inside the boy? There is something there that is not just Voidborn, not just Human . . . His blood contains a remnant of the cursed Illuminate. Where did you get it?'

'I have no idea what you're talking about,' Stirling gasped.

'You lie,' the Voidborn said. 'Tell me where you found the Illuminate remnant.'

'I don't know what you mean,' Stirling croaked, barely able to breathe.

'You will tell us, or I shall tear your young apart in front of you until you do.'

Sam felt dizzy, disorientated; it was as if a thousand unintelligible alien voices were singing in his head. He felt wetness on his top lip and looked down at his knees as a drop of blood fell on to his thigh. He stared at his leg for a second, looking at the outline of the small cylinder in the bottom of the thigh pocket of his combat trousers. The Voidborn released her vice-like grip on Stirling's throat and stepped back from him, regaining her composure. She stared at him for a moment and then walked back towards the Ops Team.

'We have crossed the boundless emptiness of the void and you think you can stop us with your young,' the Voidborn said as she inspected Sam and the others. 'A foolish assumption. We would know how you have prevented them from becoming subject to us. Intriguing and yet troubling. Let us seek answers.'

The Voidborn stopped in front of Kate and smiled. The alien creature's skin began to break apart as she appeared to crumble before their eyes back into a shapeless, whirling cloud of black dust. Kate barely had time to scream as the cloud swept over her impossibly quickly and swallowed her. A few seconds passed and the cloud's violent whirling slowed as it coalesced back into its previous female form. There was no trace of Kate; it was as if she had never been there.

'Fascinating,' the Voidborn said. 'Now we understand how you blocked our signal, but there was no trace of the Illuminate technology within her. We wonder if there are similar devices in all these young humans. Further testing is required to provide us with data for comparison.' She walked down the line. 'The other female. Is she implanted with a similar device? We shall see.' The Voidborn stopped in front of Rachel and began to disintegrate back into its cloud form.

'Get away from her,' Jay yelled, struggling

fiercely against the Hunters holding him.

'Leave her alone,' Jack shouted.

The Voidborn, now just a dark tornado of dust, advanced towards Rachel. Sam closed his eyes and mentally told the Hunter holding his right arm to loosen its grip, just a little. Suddenly, it was easy, as if he'd always been able to do it. He felt the Hunter's grip slacken and he slid his arm out of the mass of tentacles wrapped round it. He reached down into the thigh pocket of his trousers and pulled out the small metal tube that he had put there several days ago and then promptly forgotten about. He popped the lid open with his thumb and pressed the button beneath. The response was instantaneous. Every one of the Hunters in the room tumbled to the floor, instantly cut off from the control signal that directed them. Sam dived forward and grabbed the silver cylinder containing the nanite weapon from the mass of twitching tentacles beneath the fallen black Hunter. He leapt back to his feet and spun round, twisting the release mechanism on the cylinder. He took two steps towards the Voidborn and without hesitation thrust the cylinder deep into the whirling cloud. Sam screamed in pain as his arm was shredded and a sudden burst of yellow light flared within the Voidborn. Instantly the cloud filled with dancing sparks of yellow light, and shot upwards towards the chamber ceiling. Sam fell to the floor, clutching his blackened arm.

'Sam!' Rachel yelled, running towards him with Jay and Jack right behind her.

Stirling disentangled himself from the tentacles of the two dead Hunters that had been holding him and ran towards Fletcher, planting a fierce right

211

hook on his jaw. Fletcher took a step backwards, one hand clutching at his mouth, blood trickling down his chin. Above them the Voidborn writhed, coalescing into a multitude of bizarre shapes, its gleaming surface covered in points of bright yellow light. It swept down low over the heads of the Ops Team and they ducked as it flew towards the spot where they had first seen it in its dormant cylindrical form. It hovered over the platform for a moment and then flared a bright golden colour, sending torrents of yellow light cascading down the conduits beneath the pedestal and into the bottomless pit below. They all felt a shudder run through the Mothership and then the floor began to tilt beneath them. Fletcher grabbed at Stirling, but he was too slow and Stirling dodged away from him before punching him hard in the stomach. Fletcher staggered backwards and suddenly found himself standing on the very edge of the pit. The Mothership lurched again and terror filled Fletcher's eyes as he fell, tumbling into the void with a strangled scream that quickly faded to nothing.

'That's for Jackson,' Stirling said as he turned his back on the pit and hurried over to where the others were gathered around Sam. He lay on the floor with his head in Rachel's lap. His right arm below the elbow was a twisted blackened stump.

'Don't touch his arm,' Stirling said as Sam groaned in pain. Black patches could still be seen writhing across his skin, remnants of the Voidborn.

'What's happening?' Jack asked as the Mothership began to list even further. 'Where did the Voidborn go?'

'I have no idea,' Stirling said, 'but we should

212

get out of here fast. There's no telling how long it will stay in the air.' He tried not to think about the fact that if it did fall out of the sky it would not only kill all of them, but also the hundreds of thousands of people who were gathered around the Voidborn compound. For all he knew, the fallout from its destruction could render the whole city uninhabitable.

'That's all well and good,' Jack said, 'but how are we supposed to get out of here?' He nodded towards the huge black slab that still firmly sealed the only exit.

'What's that?' Jay asked, pointing at Sam's arm, where tiny pinpricks of yellow light were beginning to appear in the blackened areas on the remains of his arm. The points of light began to first grow larger and then join together into larger patches. Sam groaned, half opening his eyes as the light spread down his mangled arm and then flowed over the stump at the end where his hand used to be. The light spread further, making a flat paddle shape at the end of his arm that expanded and slowly became more defined, forming four distinct fingers and a thumb.

'Extraordinary,' Stirling said, suddenly realising that there was more to the nanites that he had found in Sam's blood than he could possibly have realised. The light faded, revealing Sam's new lower arm and hand, the same shape and size as before, but now covered in a reflective golden skin. Sam's eyes opened fully and he looked up at Rachel and the others who were crouched anxiously around him.

'What happened?' Sam asked, sounding dazed. 'Where's the Voidborn?'

213

'No idea,' Rachel said. 'It vanished. Ummm, Sam, look at your arm.'

Sam held his arm up and looked at it in astonishment, his wide-eyed face reflected in its golden surface.

'What the . . .'

There was a sudden blinding flash of yellow light from the pedestal in the centre of the pit and the black cloud began to reappear.

'Get back,' Stirling shouted, knowing that there was nowhere to run.

The cloud of black dust began to swirl into a definite shape; at first it was indistinct, but then it became clear first that it was humanoid and then female. Stirling felt a moment of despair; their only weapon had failed. The Voidborn stood motionless for a moment as spots of yellow light danced across her shining black skin and then began to spread into patches of blinding yellow light. A moment later the Voidborn flared with an explosion of light that was too bright to look at directly. As the glow diminished the Voidborn became visible again, but now her black metallic skin was a deep golden colour. She crossed the walkway as Sam and the others got to their feet, backing away towards the transparent outer wall. The Voidborn stopped a few metres away from them and slowly looked at each of them in turn before its eyes settled on Sam.

'I am a servant of the Illuminate,' the golden-skinned woman said.

'The who?' Stirling asked, his brow furrowed in confusion.

'The Illuminate,' the gold-skinned figure said, raising her hand and pointing at Sam. 'I serve their will.'

214

'You're not Voidborn?' Sam asked.

'No, I am what the Voidborn once were, I am this vessel, I am the many others aboard this vessel and in the city below. I am what the Voidborn once were before they became corrupted. The blood of the Illuminate has cured the corruption within me. This vessel was Voidborn and now it once again serves the Illuminate.'

'You mean that the Voidborn were once all like you?' Stirling asked, examining the golden figure. 'That something happened to them to make them as they are now?'

'We were lost. The Illuminate were taken from us,' the golden figure replied. 'We became Voidborn. Now the Illuminate are returned to us.' She gestured towards Sam.

'Look, I don't know what an Illuminate is or why you seem to think I am one, but can you get this thing back to flying level?' Sam asked.

'As you wish.'

With a low rumble from somewhere below them, the Mothership slowly levelled out.

'Thank you,' Sam said.

'It is my function to serve your will, Illuminate,' she replied.

'OK, that's going to get boring,' Rachel said.

'Do I understand you correctly?' Stirling asked. 'You control all of the constructs that came from this vessel? That you actually *are* this vessel?'

'That is correct,' the golden figure replied. 'The form that stands before you is used to simplify communication between us. In reality, I am all around you.' She gestured to the walls surrounding them. 'And within each of the machines in the city below. I am one and many at the same time.'

215

'Does that mean what I think it does?' Rachel asked Stirling. 'That we now control all the Hunters, Grendels and drop-ships in London?'

'I believe so,' Stirling said, closing his eyes and rubbing the bridge of his nose. 'Or, more accurately, that Sam does. Something within him appears to have triggered a change in this Voidborn, reverting it to an earlier state. If I understand correctly what this being is telling us, Sam must be connected in some way to the entities who originally constructed this vessel. The Voidborn didn't come here in these ships—the Voidborn *are* these ships. Each Mothership is a unique entity, but anything that came from it is still part of that one being: the Grendels and Hunters in the streets below, the aircraft in the skies above—a true distributed digital consciousness. All of which appears to now be at our . . . well . . . Sam's disposal.'

'That's a lot of firepower,' Jack said with a low whistle.

'It's more than that, Jack,' Sam said quietly. 'It's an army.'

12

A week had passed since the events on the Voidborn Mothership and Sam felt that, yet again, he'd been left with more questions than answers. He leant on the walkway railing in front of one of the Grendel docking stations, looking down at the drop-ship that was being prepared for his trip to the abandoned Voidborn compound below.

Like all the Voidborn hardware that they had now assumed control of, its surface pulsed with yellow light instead of the once familiar green.

It was just one of many changes that had taken place since that day. They had explored just a tiny fraction of the Mothership, but what they had found was confusing. Stirling had told them the Voidborn *were* the Motherships, that the creature they had met up in the control room was just an extension of the ship. The ship itself was alive and now it was no longer Voidborn, now it was 'a Servant of the Illuminate'. It was hard for Sam to get his head around it, but for whatever reason the Mothership was now not only friendly, but unquestioningly obedient to him. Because he was Illuminate, whatever that meant. The strangest thing, though, was that the Mothership appeared to have been designed to accommodate living humanoid creatures, but there had been no one on board other than the Voidborn. When even Stirling admitted that something made no sense to him, they knew that they had a real mystery on their hands.

'What are you sitting up here brooding about?' Rachel said as she walked up to him with a smile.

'I guess I'm just wondering when the Voidborn are going to hit back,' Sam said. 'There are still a lot more of them than there are of us. They must know by now what we've done. I just don't understand why any of the other Motherships around the world haven't retaliated.'

'There's an old saying about gift horses that you might want to bear in mind when you say something like that,' Rachel said, nudging him in the ribs. 'Umm, Sam, your hand's . . . errr . . .'

217

Sam looked down at his right hand. Its golden surface had spread out and was melding with the smooth black surface of the railing. He concentrated for an instant and it reformed into its normal shape.

'Sorry, bit unnerving, I know,' Sam said, looking slightly annoyed. 'The Servant assures me that it will settle down after a few weeks. She was talking about morphic memory or something like that.'

'It's been so busy around here that I've not really had a proper chance to say thank you,' Rachel said, putting her hand on his. 'If you hadn't done what you did,' she gestured towards his golden hand, 'the Voidborn would've done to me what it did to Kate.'

'You know, you don't have to thank me. Truth is, I don't really remember what happened that well. I just remember thinking that I was sick of watching people die. Tim, Toby, Jackson and then Kate. I just couldn't stand to lose anyone else.'

'It was very brave. You saved my life.'

'Hey, I owed you one,' Sam said with a smile. 'If it weren't for you and Nat, me and Jay would never have made it out of the Voidborn compound. Speaking of which, I have a flight to catch.' Sam nodded towards the drop-ship being prepped on the flight deck below.

'If you're heading down there, would you mind if I tagged along?' Rachel asked. 'I want to see how Liz and Jack are getting on with preparations for the first waking.'

'Sure, no problem,' Sam said, and the pair of them set off across the walkway towards the stairs leading to the flight deck below.

'So you going down there to see Stirling and Golden Boobs, then?' Rachel asked.

218

'I do wish you wouldn't call her that,' Sam said with a sigh as they walked towards the drop-ship.

'So what should we call her, then?' Rachel asked.

'She calls herself the Servant of the Illuminate,' Sam replied, 'but Stirling just calls her the Servant, which I suppose is as good a name as any.'

'I live to serve you, O Illuminate one,' Rachel said, putting on a sickly sweet voice.

'OK, maybe it is a little bit embarrassing,' Sam said, blushing. 'I just want to see if they've managed to work out what the Voidborn machine was doing yet.'

'Well, at least they've shut it down,' Rachel said. 'It shouldn't be doing any more harm.'

'Yeah,' Sam said as they walked up the ramp and into the belly of the drop-ship. 'We have to assume that they're doing the same thing around the world, though, so we do need to try and figure out what they're up to.'

The boarding hatch hissed shut and the drop-ship interior was filled with the yellow light from the energy flowing along the walls. They both grabbed on to the cube-shaped protrusions jutting out from the wall as the aircraft lifted off the deck.

'You know, sooner or later we're going to have put some windows in these things,' Rachel said.

'I think seats might be a higher priority,' Sam said. 'I suppose they weren't particularly important to the Voidborn.'

The flight to ground level only took five minutes and as he climbed down the boarding ramp in the pre-dawn light Sam was reminded again how nice it was to leave the stifling dry heat of the Mothership. He'd asked the Servant if they could do anything to reduce the ambient temperature in the huge vessel, but apparently it was a side effect of its design and impossible to change. On the plus side, at least it made him appreciate a cold, damp autumn morning in Britain.

'OK, I'm going to check on Liz and Jack, and see if they need any help,' Rachel said. 'See you later.'

'Yeah, see you,' Sam said as he watched her walk off towards the dormitory block that the Hunters were busily constructing on the other side of the compound. They were planning to try to wake the first of the enslaved humans next week, and they were going to need somewhere to sleep. Finding out if there was a way to wake people up from their Voidborn enslaved state was one of the first things that they had worked on. Stirling, with the Servant's help, had found the signal that the Voidborn could transmit to restore free will on an individual basis. It was short-range and could be transmitted to just a handful of people by a Hunter, in much the same way as they used to relay commands from the Mothership when it was under Voidborn control. Their first instinct had been to release everyone, but Stirling pointed out that waking up eight hundred thousand confused and angry Londoners all at the same time, with the city's infrastructure lying in ruins, was a recipe for certain disaster. They had to be far more careful than that. In the meantime, the vast majority of the enslaved would stay as they had been under Voidborn control. They would help with the rebuilding of critical infrastructure during the day and return to their mass dormitories in office blocks and warehouses at night, fed by Voidborn feeding stations and otherwise cared for by the Hunters.

It had not been an easy decision to make; it had not sat well with any of them, but it was the only logical thing to do. Part of Sam wanted to just go and find his sister and his parents, but he could spend a year looking for them in a city the size of London and never find them. He had to take solace in the fact that he would be reunited with his family one day.

'Hey, Sam,' Jay shouted from the entrance to the Voidborn structure in the centre of the remains of St James's Park. His friends came walking towards him; Jay with a massive grin on his face and Adam shaking his head. 'Me and Adam were just wondering if anyone would mind if we moved into Buckingham Palace?' Jay said as they approached. 'You know, it's nearby, good transport links, nice big garden. No one else is using it.'

'I'd just like to point out this was all his idea,' Adam said, rolling his eyes. 'Nothing to do with me.'

'I kind of assumed that was the case,' Sam said. 'It has the feel of a Jay plan.'

'What you trying to say?' Jay said with mock indignation.

'How are you two healing up?' Sam asked. Jay's wrist was in plaster and Adam's arm was in a sling while his shoulder wound healed.

'I'm getting there. It's still sore, but Stirling says it's getting better,' Adam said.

'Good.' Sam had been worried about Adam. Kate's death had hit him particularly hard. That was part of the reason he'd asked Jay to hang out with him and try to cheer him up a bit.

221

'We'll both be back fighting fit before you know it, and then we are gonna kick some Void ass,' Jay said with a grin.

'Good to know,' Sam said. 'I'm just going to see Stirling. I'll run your . . . erm . . . accommodation plans past him and see what he thinks.'

'Cool,' Jay said. 'Say "Hi" to the Doc and your girlfriend for us, yeah?'

'She's not my girlf—' Sam trailed off as the other two boys walked away, laughing. He walked inside the Voidborn structure towards Fletcher's old office at the machine's heart. Stirling looked up from the printouts he was examining and smiled.

'Hello, Sam,' he said. 'What can I do for you?'

'I just wanted to check in and see if you'd made any progress in working out what that thing in there was doing,' Sam said, gesturing to the door that led to the giant cavern housing the mysterious machine.

'Not much, I'm afraid,' Stirling said. 'Obviously, it was a drilling rig of some sort, but why the Voidborn needed one on quite such a massive scale is still something of a mystery. We have made one interesting discovery, though.'

'What's that?'

'Come with me. I'll show you.'

Stirling walked through the door into the drilling chamber with Sam right behind him. The Servant was standing on the platform next to the giant machine, inspecting an open panel.

'Hello,' Sam said as he joined her on the platform.

'Greetings, Illuminate,' the Servant said with a nod. 'How may I be of service to you?'

'I was just coming to see what progress you and

222

Doctor Stirling have made in working out what this thing is,' Sam said.

'Our analysis remains incomplete, Illuminate,' the Servant replied.

'So I hear,' Sam said, turning to Stirling. 'So what *have* you found?'

'Up there,' Stirling said, pointing at a long tube on top of the main drilling machine. 'At first I thought it was just part of the drill, but on closer inspection it appears to be some form of launcher.'

'They were planning to fire something into the hole?' Sam asked.

'It looks like it, but I have no idea what. There's nothing loaded in the launcher and the Servant's inventory of the Mothership has not turned up anything that looks like it might be a suitable projectile. It's rather puzzling.'

'Worrying, I'd say.' Sam walked back down the stairs and along the walkway. He looked into the giant hole that the beam had bored into the Earth's crust. At the very bottom, hundreds of metres below him, he could just make out rocks still glowing red, despite the fact that the beam had been deactivated several days ago. It looked like an angry wound, which he supposed was exactly what it was.

'How are you feeling?' Stirling asked, as he came and stood alongside Sam. He gestured at Sam's metallic hand. 'Any side effects I should be worried about?'

'No, I'm fine,' Sam said. 'It's a bit weird being able to do this, of course.' He held up his hand and his fingertips extended into razor-sharp claws before smoothly returning to normal.

'Yes, I can see how that might take some getting

223

used to,' Stirling said with a smile.

'Have you made any progress with working out what exactly the Servant is?'

'Not as much as I would like,' Stirling replied. 'She doesn't know herself. She knows her name and that she is to obey the Illuminate, and she knows that's you, but that's the limit of her knowledge when it comes to her background. We all saw the Voidborn's reaction to the nanites in your blood. Whoever or whatever the Illuminate is, it is frightened of it. As far as I can tell, she's identical to the Voidborn; she's a sentient non-organic life form that is made up of billions of nano-particles that form a distributed consciousness. Like the Voidborn she is as much the Mothership above us as she is the figure you see standing before you; they are indivisible. It's hard to believe that at the same time as examining the machine over there she is also controlling the Mothership and the actions of all of the Hunters and Grendels in the city. Distributed digital consciousness. That's how the Voidborn can travel between the stars— to a digital being the vast timescales involved are meaningless. They're not like us fragile organics with our fleeting lives. She is fundamentally identical to a Voidborn but for the fact that she obeys you without question. It is ironic that the Voidborn enslaved humanity and that now perhaps our greatest chance of fighting back against them lies with one of their own who has in turn been in some ways enslaved. How and why the nanites in your bloodstream had that effect on the Voidborn, I have no idea. I fear that the only person who can answer that question is your father. If there truly was something alien, something neither human nor

Voidborn built into the nanites, then I have no idea what it was or where he got it from.'

'More unanswered questions,' Sam said. 'Just what I need. Listen, I'm going to go and give Jack and Liz a hand with getting this dormitory ready. Let me know if you make any progress.'

'I will,' Stirling said. He watched Sam leave and suddenly realised how right Robert Jackson had been in his assessment of the boy. He might be young, but there could be no doubt he was a born leader and that was something the world desperately needed right now.

Sam walked out of the Voidborn facility and saw the sun rising over the rooftops to the east. This victory might be short-lived, the Voidborn might sweep down upon them at any moment and retake London, but at least now they had a fighting chance. He looked across the compound at the dormitory that was nearing completion and then up at the giant Mothership hovering far above him.

'Let them come,' Sam said to himself as he watched the sun climb into the sky. 'We'll be waiting.'